# ESCAPE TO SHELTER SPRINGS

SOPHIE HAYDON

BAY BOOKS

**Escape to Shelter Springs**
by Sophie Haydon

*A woman wanting freedom. A man determined to keep his family safe and secure. A marriage doomed before it's begun...*

**—The Mackenzies—**
A Place Called Home
Secrets at Parata Bay
Escape to Shelter Springs
What you See in the Stars
Second Chance at Whisper Creek
Summer at the Lakehouse Café

**—Lantern Bay—**
Yours to Give
Yours to Treasure
Yours to Cherish
Yours to Keep
Yours Forever
Yours to Love

Find out more at https://sophiehaydon.com

ISBN 978-199-102107-6 (Amazon Print)
ISBN 978-199-102126-7 (Draft2Digital Print)
© 2013 Diana Fraser

# CONTENTS

## PROLOGUE

"Where are you going?" His voice was cold and authoritative and sent a wave of fear through Gemma.

She stopped, just steps away from the front door of the apartment, and watched his lighter flare in the dark of the bedroom, revealing only his silhouette as he sucked on the ever-present cigarette. She was prepared for his question. Paul always insisted on knowing where she was going and with whom.

"I need to buy new stockings for tonight." Paul couldn't stand imperfections—not ladders in stockings, or in people—and Gemma prayed he wouldn't insist on going with her. "I won't be long."

"You're not going alone." His hand shot out from the darkened bedroom and gripped her tightly around the wrist. She gasped, but before he could emerge into the hall, his cell phone rang. He hesitated briefly before releasing her and disappearing inside the room to answer the phone. She exhaled her tightly held breath and wasted no time in exiting the apartment.

Once in the marble lobby she pressed the elevator button and waited. She gripped the small bag that held all her belongings, willing him not to appear.

After what seemed an age, the elevator arrived. She pressed the button for the basement and turned to look at the apartment for the last time. The elevator doors slid closed on her life for the past three years—a life that had been full of comfort and security at first but which had proved to be suffocating and terrifying in the finish.

She walked past her car and out through the rear exit onto the busy street towards where her taxi was waiting.

"Heathrow, please."

She closed her eyes and kept them closed against the regular flash of the streetlights. Only her friend, Sarah, knew where she was going, and she had her own reasons for never divulging Gemma's whereabouts.

It was time to disappear, time to make a new start... time to breathe again.

# CHAPTER ONE

*Forty hours later...*

Gemma jumped out of the rental car, strode away from the river, up to the grassy knoll and looked around. Great. One day in New Zealand and she was spectacularly lost.

Despite being lost, Gemma breathed in the chill, fresh air and smiled to herself. She'd done it! She'd wriggled out from her boyfriend's grasp and found herself a new life. Or she would have, once she'd worked out where she was.

Since she'd crossed the river, there had been nothing to see but mile after mile of tussock grass leading to mountains she knew to exist from the map, but whose snow-topped summits had been shrouded in heavy cloud since she'd landed. There was no sign of life, no sign of mountains and certainly no sign of the homestead Sarah had said she could stay in. She knew it was in the middle of nowhere, but this was ridiculous.

Gemma shook out the map and turned it around, trying to figure out where she was in relation to the wiggly contour lines. But a large drop of rain splattered onto it, making it instantly unreadable. It was quickly followed by others and she looked up in time to see the wall of gray cloud that had been hovering in the mountains all afternoon, rapidly descending on her. She leaped back into the car, switched on the light and tried to figure out where to go next.

Suddenly the palm of a hand slapped against the outside of the window. Gemma screamed as the same hand grabbed hold of the door handle. She tried to press down the lock, but her cold fingers fumbled with the button which slid from under her grasp as the door was yanked open.

"You need to come with me. *Now!*" The male voice was commanding and urgent.

*What the hell? Had she been followed here? Had Paul tracked her down already?*

"No way!" She tried to pull the door closed but a hand pulled her arm from the door.

"Come on! We don't have much time."

"Hey! Let go! I'm not going anywhere with you!"

The dark figure bent down then and she saw it belonged to a cowboy—or maybe not—this *was* New Zealand after all. She strained to see his face in the gray light, but his battered bushman's hat was pulled low to keep the rain off his face. All that was visible was a strong jaw line covered with a day's worth of stubble.

"Come on!" he repeated. "There's no time to argue."

"No!" She tried once more to pull the door closed but the man huffed, reached inside and slid one hand under her while grabbing her bag with the other and pulled her to him. She screamed and pushed her hands flat against his chest, trying to pry herself from his grip. But he was too strong. He picked her up and strode away. She screamed again, twisting in his tight embrace, and kicked him hard. He groaned but didn't miss a step.

"Quieten down." He slung her over his shoulder in a fireman's hold and the air rushed from her body. All she could do was gasp for breath, all she could see was the rain, hammering into the soil, turning it into a sea of slick, gray mud, and all she could feel was the grip of his hands, tight around her legs. And all she could think was that Paul had found her and she was a dead woman. No one walked away from Paul.

Within minutes the man had stopped, opened the door of a Range Rover and tossed her and her bag inside, just as an almighty clap of thunder echoed around the wide valley. Before Gemma could move, he'd clicked a lock in the side of the door so she couldn't escape and had jumped into the driver's seat and roared off as if the devil was after them. She backed into the corner and looked around as she tried to regain her breath.

He glanced at her with ice-blue eyes as hard and cold as the land outside. "I won't hurt you."

"Then let me go." Her voice sounded strangled.

"Can't do that. We have to get out of here—*now*."

The SUV revved loudly as it moved up over steep ground away from the river. She barely heard her words of protest above the hammering of the rain on the roof and the spinning of the wheels as they tried to gain traction in the mud.

Suddenly he slammed on the brakes, turned to her and pushed up his hat. For the first time Gemma saw his face properly. Her first impressions were confirmed. He was just like the country around them. The bone structure of his face was strong and powerful, his expression as unforgiving and impressive as the mountains that ringed the huge valley. She shivered and pressed herself back against the door.

His eyes flickered over her face. "Look down there."

Gemma had no inclination to take her eyes off him. "Why would I do that? Give you another chance to attack me? I'm not going with you, I'm not going back to him."

He shook his head. "What the hell are you talking about, woman? Just look down there."

Her heart hammered, but as she continued to stare at him, she felt strangely reassured. Perhaps this man wasn't one of Paul's men. He didn't appear to be like his sort. She didn't get the *feeling* he was.

"Just look," he repeated.

She nodded slowly, let out a tight breath and peered through the window, down to the river below. "At what?" She rubbed the condensation off the window just in time to see a wall of water descend the river. It spilled over the banks, washed away the bridge she'd just crossed, scooped up her hire car and swept it along the valley. "Oh..." She couldn't believe what she was seeing. She cleared the window of condensation again and took another look at the place she'd been standing only minutes earlier that was now flooded by surging gray water. "My car! My things... Oh. My. *God!* What the hell was that?"

"A fresh. It's been raining in the hills for days. One was due any time."

Gemma sat back, stunned, her eyes fixed on the receding car, bobbing black on the gray surge of the river, as it disappeared into a watery landscape of cloud, mist and rain. Her heart still thumped from being manhandled by a stranger, but her fear had now changed into the shock of having narrowly escaped death.

"What am I going to do? All I had in the world was in that car."

"It'll wash up downriver somewhere. We'll find it later, but not now." He slipped the SUV into gear and accelerated up the uneven slope once more.

"But we *have* to. We *have* to go and look for it."

"We're on the wrong side of the river for town. I crossed the river to get to you. Now the bridge's gone, the nearest passable crossing is a day away."

As they took off into the unknown, Gemma fixed her shocked gaze on the wet, gray world, revealed by the regular slap of the windshield wipers. The vehicle skidded, and she held her breath as it found its grip and pulled itself up a steep bank.

"But surely you must live nearby. We can go there and phone for help."

"Not this side of the river, I can't."

"Then what the hell are we going to do?"

He shifted the SUV into first gear. "Find shelter."

She pressed her palm against her forehead, willing it all to go away. *This wasn't how it was meant to be.* She'd come here to find freedom and everything—nature and man—was conspiring to trap her again.

"You mean there *is* somewhere we can go?"

"The river will be impassable for at least twenty-four hours. But there's an old shepherd's hut, not too far away, which I keep stocked for emergencies."

*A shepherd's hut, twenty-four hours, a stranger.* The words played over and over in her mind like a nightmarish chant.

"Well, I'm guessing this sure counts as an emergency."

"I reckon. What the hell are you doing out here anyway?"

She chewed her lip with indecision. She hated lies but she couldn't risk Paul finding her. If she was going to pose as heiress of Blackrock she may as well start now. She and Sarah had decided Gemma could get away with using her own name as the owner's identity was hidden behind a screen of companies. Only the Auckland lawyers knew the truth and it was more than their reputation was worth to reveal it.

"I've just landed from the UK. My family used to live here a long time ago. Thought I'd check out my family history."

"Strange place to do it."

"Strange family by all accounts."

"Aren't they all?"

"So what were *you* doing out here?"

"Checking on stock. Just as well, otherwise you'd be gone."

*Gone.* She closed her eyes tight. She would have been, too. All this way to find a new life and it had nearly ended before it'd begun. "Thank God for stock." She took a deep breath and looked at him. "Thank you. I thought you were crazy, I thought you were going to attack me."

His eyes were narrowed and his mouth clamped tight in concentration as he swung the car around, avoiding rocks and potholes as best he could. Her eyes lingered on his lips, firm yet quite full. Soft even. He glanced at her and she swallowed and turned back to the window. She was suddenly acutely aware they were quite alone together—no one around for miles.

"No. On both counts."

"I'm glad about that, since we'll be spending the next few hours together."

"Put your seat belt on."

Instinctively Gemma began to frame words of objection. She hadn't traveled ten thousand miles to be ordered around, controlled—that's what she'd come here to escape from—but the car suddenly struck a ridge and it flew into the air before landing with a sharp bump.

"Just do it."

She didn't need telling again.

The storm intensified. Rain descended like steel bullets and lightning sparked the leaden sky. Thunder crashed around them, hardly settling before enveloping them in a fresh roll. Gemma wedged herself in the seat, trying to stop herself from being thrown around as they lurched over rough tussock towards higher ground. At last they slowed and he swung the car through a narrow opening in a small copse of gnarled, wind-battered trees in the midst of which an old cob cottage stood.

"This is it."

She turned to him at the same moment as a flash of lightning silhouetted his profile. He didn't look human in that eerie light. His face could have been hewn from granite. It was so strong, so hard, unfeeling. Then the moment passed and he was out of the vehicle and lost in the stream of rain that washed over the windows. She grabbed her bag and jumped out into the mud after him. Head down, she stumbled across the small yard onto a narrow verandah and slapped right into him. He threw the door open wide and pushed her inside. The wind slammed the door closed behind them.

"Okay?"

She shrugged. Where should she begin? Lost? Frozen? Terrified?

"Good." He opened the door once more, obviously taking her silence for the affirmative. "I won't be long." The door slammed shut behind him, leaving Gemma alone in the strangely quiet cottage. She stepped into the gloom and looked around. Her heart sank. A shepherd's needs were obviously minimal as there was little in the hut except a bed, table, two chairs and a stove—all in the one room. A half-open door revealed the edge of a bath. She heaved a sigh of relief.

Before she had time to explore further, a gust of wind blew into the room as the man entered, his dark form outlined by the lighter iron-gray of the sky outside.

"I guess you haven't found the lamp yet."

He nudged the door closed with his foot, dropped a pile of logs on the floor and strode through to the rear of the small hut.

Gemma relaxed as the hiss of gas ignited and the small flame grew as he replaced the shade. As he brought the lantern to the only table, she opened the potbelly stove and peered inside.

"Get the fire going, will you? I'll get some more wood."

He disappeared outside once more and Gemma heard the thud of logs being shifted against the rear of the cottage. She opened the lid to the stove, dropped a few logs in and sighed. This wasn't exactly what she'd envisioned as she and Sarah had devised Gemma's plan of escape. She struck a match and dropped it on top of the logs. As the man re-entered the room, the spark bloomed momentarily before immediately dying.

"What the hell are you doing, woman?" He dropped the second armful of logs onto the floor and took off his coat, the rain pooling on the bare wooden boards.

"Trying to light a fire."

He withdrew the logs from the stove and tore off some

of the outer bark and twigs to make kindling. "Something you've never done before, at a guess."

"You guess right. Not much call for lighting fires in London."

"Perhaps you should have stuck to London." He shot her an irritated glance. "Saved us both from an uncomfortable night."

Gemma looked away, suddenly aware that he was right. If it weren't for her, he'd no doubt be happily back at his home by now, wherever that was. "Hey, I'm sorry. But, I've done with London. I've come to New Zealand looking for something different." The truth. That felt better.

He turned away from the weak flame that had just caught in the stove and looked at her then, as if for the first time. He didn't look at her like any of the men she'd known before. This was no sly assessment. He checked her out openly. She imagined he'd do the same for any stock he'd buy. He glanced down at her sodden jeans that clung to her legs, and then up, over her wet fleece before his gaze came to rest on her hair that had escaped her beanie. There he stopped, for a moment too long. She lifted her hand to her hair and pushed some wet strands off her face. Her movement seemed to break the spell and he turned away.

"Well," he said slowly, "something different all right."

She frowned. His words, that should have been a simple reply to her comment, were uttered slowly, thoughtfully, as if he meant something else entirely. She watched as he turned his attention back to the fire, opening the damper and coaxing the flames higher until they engulfed the kindling, before dropping in one of the smaller logs. He took off his hat and tossed it onto the table, pushing his hands through sun-streaked hair before turning back to look at her again.

Attraction bloomed from somewhere deep within, making her heart pound and heat spread throughout her body. She looked away quickly, confused. She'd never had such an instant reaction to someone and she didn't want one now.

"You'd better get yourself out of those clothes. You'll find some towels in the cupboard."

"Sure." She plucked off her soaking beanie and tossed it to one side. She shook out her hair and turned to find him staring at her.

"You have red hair."

Her confusion deepened when she saw his expression. She nodded. She had to keep it light. "Yeah, the original ginger, that's me. Ginger and very wet hair." He shook his head, frowned and turned away. "Look," she sighed. "I'm cold. I think I'll go and have a shower, if that's okay." She unzipped her fleece.

"No."

"But," she smiled patiently, "I'd like one now." She plucked at her saturated clothes.

"Not yet."

He stood up. She wished he hadn't. Her eyes were on a level with his chest, visible through the open neck of his shirt. She swallowed and lifted her chin to meet his gaze. It was equally determined. There would be no argument. He was obviously used to getting his own way. But not this time, not with this woman. She'd had enough of being ordered around.

She took a step closer to him, trying to hide the flutter of nerves. "And why not?"

"Because we've got no hot water until the fire's warmed it. Shower later, but you need to get out of those clothes now." His gaze traveled the length of her body.

Her skin tingled and she folded her arms across her breasts, suddenly aware of how her wet clothes revealed the flood of sensations that swept through her.

"You should find whatever you want in the cupboard," he added.

"Right." She opened the cupboard and pried open the lid of a huge chest. "Is there anything you haven't got in here?" She pulled out a towel and continued to explore the chest. "Spices, biscuits, caviar, pasta, whisky."

"I could do with a glass of that now."

She passed him the bottle and some glasses, grabbed the towel and padded over to the bathroom, leaving a trail of wet footprints behind her.

"You'd be better off stripping in front of the fire. You'll freeze your butt off in the bathroom."

Rather a frozen butt than an exposed one, she thought. "I'll survive."

"Then there's the mice."

Gemma stopped dead in her tracks. "Mice?"

"Sure. Why do you think I keep everything in the chest?" He twisted off the lid and poured two generous glasses of whisky before passing one to her.

"Mice?" she repeated. The chills that ran down her spine had nothing to do with her soaking clothes.

"Yep. They can't get into the chest but the rest of the place is fair game." He gave her a wry smile. "Especially the bathroom."

Gemma sat down quickly. She hated mice. Hated them. From their soft furry bodies to their long slithering tails. She looked up at him suspiciously. Was he having her on? Trying to get her to strip in front of him?

"The rain could bring them inside in droves." He passed her the glass of whisky.

"You're doing this on purpose."

He shrugged. "Get changed in the bathroom if you want to."

She took a big gulp of her whisky and coughed as it hit her throat before igniting a fiery trail down to her stomach. "I think I'll pass on the mouse-infested bathroom."

"Come over here by the fire and I'll get us some food. You like pasta?"

"Yes. Love it."

He extended his hand as she approached the stove. "A bit late, but I'm Callum Mackenzie."

She took his hand. "Gemma Winters."

"Gemma Winters." He rolled the syllables around his mouth as if he was tasting them. "So, Gemma Winters, why choose the Mackenzie country to explore your family tree? Why not Christchurch library? They have electricity there, I believe. Heaters even." He grinned for the first time and she melted.

"Very funny."

"Seriously, why here?"

She looked at him suspiciously. She was in for a long night. She didn't want to bare her soul. She didn't want to tell him her life story and she couldn't face telling any more lies. "It's a long story."

"We have a long night ahead."

"Tell me about you first."

He shrugged. "Sure. I'm *from* here—born and bred. This is my country." He downed his whisky in one gulp and took both glasses to refill them, topping hers up with the hot water that had just boiled on the stove.

"I guessed you were. You look like you belong here."

"Just as you look like you belong in London."

She shook her head. "Not any more. I've been left a

house here somewhere by a distant cousin. It's called Black-rock. Doesn't sound inviting and I haven't found it yet. But whatever's it's like will be fine with me."

"Blackrock," Callum repeated, frowning.

"Yes, do you know it?"

"Yep. You must have passed it before you crossed the river. I'm not surprised you didn't see it—it's lost amongst the trees now. It's pretty derelict and it's not livable."

"I don't care what state it's in, I'm living there."

His lips tightened thoughtfully. "You'd be better off letting the house fall down and selling the land. Won't be of any use to you in the middle of nowhere."

Gemma hesitated. Sarah had told her she wasn't able to sell the land because of the house. It was some bizarre condition of the will. "How do you know about the caveat on the will?"

"It's common knowledge. The owner was eccentric with a grudge against people round here. Didn't want it sold to anyone who might actually profit from it." His mouth tightened more grimly. "Anyhow, what plans do you have for the place?"

She shrugged. "I don't know. I need to see it first. If it's in as bad a state of repair as you say, I'll need to fix it up."

"You'll need money for that. Do you have any?"

She shook her head. "I'll get a job."

"Do you have permanent residency?"

"Not yet. I'm on a visitor's visa, but my work doesn't usually involve much paperwork."

"What kind of work do you do?"

"I'm a waitress." Or at least she had been before she'd met Paul.

"I'll ask around for you."

"Thanks."

Gemma suddenly felt uncomfortable. He was looking at her in a different way since she'd mentioned Blackrock. "So, how long will this last—the storm, that is?"

"Hard to tell. Twelve to twenty-four hours. We'll be here for a night at least."

"Right." She eyed the lone double bed warily.

He'd followed her gaze. "Uncomfortable with that?"

"Well, I just wondered... what the sleeping arrangements were going to be. Where should I sleep?"

He nodded to the bed. "In there."

"But...what about you? Where will you sleep?"

"In there—with you."

"Well, hang on a minute. I don't know what you take me for but I'm not in the habit of sleeping with strangers."

A smile flickered on his lips. "Perhaps you mistook my meaning. It wasn't an invitation for sex, just sleep."

"Er, right. Of course." She guessed it wasn't too late to learn that there were men out there *not* like Paul, men who saved her from disaster and who didn't expect sex in return.

"You go ahead and strip while I make the bed." Again the little tweak at the corner of his mouth. "I promise not to look."

Perhaps he didn't expect sex, but he was certainly enjoying the situation. She watched him closely as she pulled the huge towel loosely around her, clutching it with one hand while she peeled off the soaking jeans with the other.

Just the sight of him making the bed was enough to divert her mind from her predicament. His shirtsleeves were rolled up now the cottage was warm, revealing a haze of golden hairs on his tanned arms, covering the contours of his bunched muscles. And then there were his hands, large, strong and, she knew from experience, capable.

Somehow she managed to slip off her t-shirt and keep the towel in place. She threw it on top of her wet jeans. Then she looked down at her soaking underwear and across at Callum who'd found some pillows from a cupboard and had tossed them on the bed. Should she leave her underwear on? Soaking wet, she felt the chill of them in contrast to the warmth of her exposed skin. No choice.

She didn't let her gaze leave Callum. She couldn't—it was the only way she could make sure he didn't watch her. But her eyes dropped from his face, noticing the way his shirt hung from broad shoulders and fell over his faded jeans, which were soaked where his coat had failed to cover them.

She kicked away her bra and panties, hiding them under the rest of her sodden clothes. She was naked now under the towel.

She watched as he flung the large duvet onto the bed. There was a control and restraint about his movements, made all the more impressive by his obvious strength. He didn't look like the kind of man you'd want to get on the wrong side of. She knew his name now but he was still a stranger. She just hoped that by morning he would still be a stranger.

Callum sat back in the hard upright chair, took a mouthful of whisky, stretched out his legs in front of him and watched Gemma hop about, as she clutched a towel and shot him furtive looks. He probably shouldn't have told her about the mice but he was glad he had. It wasn't a lie exactly. Just because he'd never seen any, it didn't mean there weren't any. And to think all he had planned was a quiet night working on the accounts. What was that saying about an ill wind? Whatever it was, it was wrong.

The heiress of Blackrock. Perfect, in so many ways. She bent over to push the mound of wet clothes out of his sight and he grinned. There was something intriguingly innocent about her. She was trying to hide her underwear while at the same time pushing out her behind. He narrowed his eyes as he focused on her bottom, nicely rounded despite her slim figure. And her hair. She'd described it as ginger but that didn't begin to describe the depth of color. It was like... His mind groped for words to describe what it was like. A copper beech in autumn? The tawny sheen of his favorite stallion after a brisk gallop? No, her hair wasn't like dying leaves or a sweaty horse. He sighed. He'd never been good with words.

All he knew was her hair was just right—despite his life-long love of blondes—and she had curves in all the right places. That she was the new owner of Blackrock—land his family had coveted for two generations since his grandfather had lost it in a gambling session—only added to her attractions. It was going to be an interesting night.

# CHAPTER TWO

Callum frowned in concentration as he sent a text, his large fingers stabbing the phone. Gemma took advantage of the momentary distraction to admire the strong planes of his face, shadowed in the muted light. She had a curious feeling she knew what it would feel like to run her fingers lightly over his stubble-roughened skin—stimulating and yet quieting at the same time. She shivered in anticipation.

He looked up and caught her watching him. Her stomach contracted and a thrill ripped through her body as his eyes, dark in the dim light, narrowed.

"Cold?"

"A little." But it wasn't cold that made her shiver. Watching him had stirred a desire she'd never felt with Paul.

"Umm, I can see that."

His voice was a low rumble that she felt through her body, as much as heard. She was overwhelmed by a compulsion to run her hand down his strong neck to his chest, revealed by the open shirt—tanned, sprinkled with golden hair. She had a sudden impulse to press down on the springy hair and feel the heat and muscle that lay beneath. She remembered his masculine smell when he'd held her tight to his body. Her body responded. She wanted to smell him again.

"You might feel warmer when you're dressed."

She tightened the towel. "Sure." She took a deep breath. She had to get a grip. He was a man, like any other, and she hadn't come to New Zealand to find a man. "Any suggestions? My clothes are all soaked."

He rose slowly and walked towards her, his eyes fixed on hers, a small smile curling at his lips. What was he going to do? Rip off her towel? Warm her with his body? But she didn't run away as she should have done. She stood still, and waited. His grin broadened as he walked past her and opened the cupboard. He took out a t-shirt and tossed it to her.

"Try this for size. Not much point giving you a pair of my jeans."

She let the breath she was holding slide out of her body. She shook her head. She was losing the plot. "Thanks." She slipped it on. It was huge. Only her breasts stopped it falling off completely, but at least it covered from her knees up. She yanked up both shoulders and let the towel drop to the floor. "It's, er, better than nothing."

He grinned and turned to the stove—pouring a stream of pasta into the now bubbling water. His smile continued to play around his lips and she felt a blush rise through her body as she imagined the cause of the smile.

"Okay. I'll let you make the sauce—there's plenty of ingredients—while I check everything's secure outside and get changed."

"Right then." She smiled hesitantly, wondering how on

earth she was going to make a sauce when she hadn't the first idea how to cook.

"Umm."

There was something in the way that Callum uttered the word—through a mouth that was glued together with a determination not usually seen when eating—that made Gemma look up to see his brows knitted together.

"Anything wrong?"

"No. I'm just wondering how long you boiled the pasta for?"

Gemma frowned as she tried to recall. "Not sure. Twenty minutes or so."

"'Or so' being another ten or more minutes judging by the consistency." Callum's lips curled as he pressed down with his fork onto a layer of pasta that disintegrated into one mushy lump.

"Yeah." She frowned and stirred her own plate of congealed mess. "At least."

"Right." He raised his eyebrows as if trying to understand something before lowering them and bracing himself for another mouthful. "I take it that, as well as not being able to light a fire, you can't cook either."

She sighed and pushed the plate away, relieved she didn't have to pretend any more. "Unfortunately not. Sorry about that." She twisted her mouth in an effort to suppress a smile. It mustn't have worked because she saw an answering grin in Callum. He pushed his plate away too.

"Just as well I had a big lunch." He sat back in his chair and looked at her consideringly. "You know, not many people can get away without cooking unless they're rich or spoiled. Which one are you?"

"I *was* rich."

"Figures."

"Why?"

"No sense. Driving into a storm and nearly killing yourself."

"That's not lack of sense, that's just..."

"Ignorance?"

"Yes, I suppose so."

"So, are you returning to your rich family now you've lost everything?"

"No, I'm not rich any more. That all changed when my father died. Now all I have is in that bag."

He frowned. "Is there no one who can help you?"

She took her plate to the ancient sink. It was always easier to tell people that she had no family, if she didn't face them, if she didn't see their pity. "No, no one." She turned and crossed her arms. She was surprised to see he had no sappy look of sympathy on his face. "Besides, I don't need help. I'll find a job, I've got somewhere to live, I can sort myself out."

"Blackrock, you said." Callum sat back in the chair, the light of the flickering fire warming his steely blue gaze. "You mean to live there? The house hasn't been lived in for years."

She frowned. It was what Sarah had been afraid of. "Is it habitable?"

He shrugged. "No, you'd be best off letting it fall to ruin. Move into town."

She shook her head. "No. I can work on it. Blackrock's where I want to be." Away from prying eyes, she wanted to add, but couldn't. Suddenly she felt very tired. She pushed her hair from her face and yawned and sat down once more.

"It's been a long day for you. You should get to bed."

Bed. It lifted the veil the warmth and whisky had created. "You've no idea." She leaned back, tossed her hair over the back of the chair so it could dry better, and closed her eyes.

"You have beautiful hair, Gemma."

She opened her eyes to see his gaze travel down its length.

"Thanks." Suddenly uncomfortable, she coiled it into a knot and stuffed it into the t-shirt. "I usually wear it tied back."

"It'll dry better loose."

Despite her better judgment she found herself letting her hair fall back over the chair.

He moved his chair closer to her, stretching out his long, muscular legs in front of the fire—his faded jeans pulling tightly across his thighs—and took another drink of whisky. She hastily took another sip of hers in an effort to distract herself from the disturbing effect of his nearness, and kept her eyes focused on the swirling amber liquid.

Callum Mackenzie wasn't like anyone she'd met before. He was a physical man who made no attempt to hide behind a veneer of politeness. What you saw was what you got. With Paul, everything had been hidden—dangerous, treacherous, like shifting sands beneath a calm, beautiful sea.

But it wasn't only Callum's physicality. It was the way he made her feel that signaled his difference from Paul. When Callum turned his blue eyes to hers, he was looking, *really* looking at her, and her body responded to his interest of its own accord.

She felt his eyes on her now. She tried to contain the acceleration of her heart, tried to keep her breathing steady, tried to keep in check her wayward thoughts. Instead she licked her suddenly dry lips and turned to find his gaze resting on her. It wasn't an intense gaze, it was honest, interested, very interested. They didn't move for long seconds. She had no idea what he was thinking but if it was anything like what she was thinking, she was in trouble.

"We should go to bed."

He *was* thinking her thoughts.

"You go to bed first. I want my hair to dry." She couldn't care one way or the other about her hair but she couldn't bring herself to jump into bed with him yet because she didn't trust herself.

He nodded, a half-smile curling around his lips as if aware of what she was doing. "Right."

The chair scraped back on the wooden floor as he pushed himself up and walked towards the bed. Still facing her, he stripped off his shirt and t-shirt together. Her eyes widened in fascination and she looked away quickly and stared at the fire. She heard him unzip the fly of his jeans and, before she could stop herself, she looked up once more.

She was met with a lazy smile and the sight of his stomach, ridged with muscle below a broad chest, tanned and golden. The golden hair that covered his chest narrowed over his stomach and tailed down into his jeans, the zip of which now lay open.

She turned away quickly. "Sorry, I..."

"No need to apologize. You can watch all you want."

She shook her head and put her hand to the side of her face for good measure. "Thank you, but no. I didn't mean to, you know, watch you."

"Night then. Oh, and before you come to bed, you'll need to damp the fire down."

*Damp the fire down? He must have mistaken her for someone who knew what she was doing.*

"Sure. I'll just. Umm." She stood up and peered at the fire expectantly until she heard him sigh and step towards her.

"Come on, move out the way. I'll do it."

She moved and then she saw the sweep of his back curving into his jeans, which rested on his hips. Firelight flickered on the muscles, carving out hollows, as he maneuvered the damper. She swallowed hard, pressing her hand to her thudding heart and turned to look the other way.

"That should do it."

She turned back to him again. Despite the warmth in his eyes, her gaze fell to his body, muscled by sheer hard work, richly tanned and gleaming in the firelight. Her fingers itched to touch him, to press her hand flat against his tight stomach and lower, to where the top button lay open. She shouldn't look, she shouldn't. But her eyes didn't seem able to rise from the fly of his jeans that grew tighter as she watched, until a definite hardened form pressed against it.

She suddenly realized what was happening and looked away as a hot blush swept her body.

"Gemma, we're alone and you're a very beautiful woman. I'd be inhuman if I didn't react to you. But I'm not going to act on it unless you want me to. Okay?"

She shook her head, still unable to look him in the eye. "I don't..." She shrugged not knowing what to say. "I won't..."

"Sure."

She kept her head down, acutely aware of his movements as he stepped out of his jeans. The wooden bed creaked as he got into it. Her heart settled into a rapid beat that didn't let up even as she closed her eyes, trying to rid her mind of the image of his semi-naked body. But, somehow, the image only intensified. She opened her eyes once more and focused on the flames that surged and retreated, searching for the oxygen it had just been deprived of.

*What the hell was she going to do?* She was no innocent virgin but just the thought of getting into bed with him made her blush. She was determined to wait until she couldn't keep her eyes open.

Slowly the fire died down to a steady glow, allowing a chill to seep into her body and darkening the room so she could no longer see him. But she could hear his deep and steady breathing. She assumed he was asleep. She shivered at the sound of the wind that gathered in the trees around the hut, whining and shrieking like the stirring of lost souls.

A huge yawn wracked her body. Her watch might be telling her it was only eleven, but she'd missed a night's sleep and she was exhausted.

He sounded fast asleep. Quietly she rose, spread out her clothes before the fire to dry and tiptoed over to the bed. She lifted the duvet and gently crept in beside him. She wasn't touching him and the duvet was huge.

She lay completely still, staring up at the roughly plastered ceiling, intersected by dark, shadowy beams from which thick strands of cobwebs hung, watching the last of the firelight flicker over its surface. She shivered. She'd been stupid to sit out in the chilled room for so long. She was so cold and she felt his warmth just beside her. Out of reach. She battled the shivers that ran through her body until sleep slowly overtook her. But it wasn't long before the chill dreams of early sleep gave way to ones of warmth and comfort.

Gemma awoke with a start and felt him against her. Somehow she'd managed to move away from the edge of the bed and was now curled up in his arms, her back pressed against his chest, and her bottom? It was pressed against the soft material of his shorts and something else. And her t-shirt, rather than covering her, had ridden up high around her waist. How was she going to get herself out of this?

She tried to wriggle away but his arm tightened its hold around her waist pulling her hard against him and he moaned lightly in his sleep. Slowly she brushed her fingers over his, before clasping their tips and pulling them gently from her body. She managed to slip his hand off her stomach and pull his arm away. But his hand slid under her t-shirt and came to a full stop on her breast.

She closed her eyes and drew in a sharp breath as powerful sensations coursed through her body. She didn't dare move, but felt her nipples harden against his calloused palm. He sighed, moving closer to her, his hand rubbing her nipple as he stirred in his sleep. She arched her neck back and opened her eyes once more. She should jump up, get away from his touch. She should...but she didn't. Was he still asleep? She waited, listening to his regular breathing. He wasn't moving now, but his hand grazed her sensitive breast every time she moved slightly.

She moved again—on purpose this time—and couldn't prevent a groan of pleasure emerging from her lips.

His breathing didn't alter. His hand stayed where it was but something hard pressed into the soft flesh of her bottom. She gasped and wriggled away from him, nearly falling out of bed in the process. She stood up as he propped himself up on one arm.

"You said... you said you'd leave me alone."

"And I did. It was you who couldn't keep away from me. My body reacts, like it or not." He grinned. "And you didn't seem to mind."

"I *thought* you were asleep."

"I'm a light sleeper, particularly when I have a beautiful woman in my arms." He sighed. "Come on, it's still too early to get up. Come back to bed, I promise your virtue will be safe with me."

She didn't believe him. Since when had any man she'd known ever done what he'd said he'd do?

"It's okay. I'll sit it out here." She pushed two chairs together.

"Now, you know I won't let you. If you insist on doing that, it'll be me who's forced to be the one out of bed, trying to sleep on those two chairs."

"No, I—"

"Is forcing me to sleep on a chair any way to repay me for saving your life?"

"Well..." He had her there. She shook her head.

"Trust me, Gemma. Get back into bed and sleep."

He shifted to the far side of the bed and she climbed back in, careful to keep a good distance between them. He turned his back to her and slowly she began to relax, her eyes growing heavy and closing as she drifted into an unquiet sleep, full of dreams of water, wind, fire and passion.

---

The gray tones of dawn had already begun to filter through the shuttered windows when Gemma awoke, feeling blissfully rested despite the raw nature of her dreams. She stretched and was suddenly aware her head was supported by Callum's arm. She shifted around to look at him but he was fast asleep.

He lay on his back, one arm by his side and the other

under her head. She'd been using it as a pillow. It was a wonder his arm hadn't gone to sleep. They'd been close again, but not so close that her bottom had been bumped up against his groin, thank God. But still... The sense of being cradled in his strong arms warmed her, made her feel more secure than she'd felt for a long time.

She didn't know how long she lay, watching the strong lines of his face become imperceptibly clearer as the light grew. But it was long enough to realize how different he was from Paul in every way. Paul would never have been so courteous, so caring as this stranger. But it wasn't just that. Seeing his chest, rising and falling, the golden hairs, the dark nipples, the tanned skin, made her skin prickle with awareness, sharpened her senses, made her drink in the warm, deliciously male smell of him, made her body shiver with desire...

She should jump out of bed. Now. She should get up. The storm had blown itself out. There was no sound outside. She could rise, get dressed and they could be on their way. Now. But she didn't move. No matter what her brain told her to do, she stayed, unable to tear herself away.

She watched as his eyes flickered open, the dark lashes brushing upwards as he first looked up at the ceiling. She watched as the shadows of sleep slowly disappeared and he turned to face her with his characteristic deliberate movement. His lips slowly curved into a smile and in his eyes she saw a reflection of her own desire. And she knew then, that she wasn't going to get out of bed.

"You're still here." His voice was a sexy rumble that vibrated through her skin, thrilling and warming her deep inside. She shifted her hips instinctively.

She nodded.

"And you've been watching me sleep?" His smiled increased.

She nodded again.

"Can't have been exciting."

She swallowed. "Exciting? Well, I..." She couldn't deny it entirely, seeing as how her body had reacted so intensely.

He narrowed his gaze. "Or was it?" He shifted to his side, his arm still under her head. They lay, looking into each other's eyes for a few moments. He pushed her hair back from her face and traced her cheek with his finger. She watched as his eyes followed the path of that finger, its calloused pad leaving a faintly scratchy path that ratcheted up her responses even further. When his finger came to rest on her mouth she opened it and licked her lips. The tip of her tongue touched his finger and suddenly his gaze lifted and held hers.

Slowly, so slowly, he moved his face to hers and touched her lips with his own. She gasped and he pulled away immediately. Her gaze dropped to his mouth.

"I'm sorry, Gemma." She shook her head, not under-standing. "Why don't you get out of bed, take the first shower."

She frowned and cupped her hand around his head and brought that mouth, which was talking too much, back against her own. She felt the slight smile against her lips as he kissed her harder this time. She held her breath as all her thoughts and feelings focused on the movement of his lips against hers. His groan rumbled against her mouth and reverberated through her body, fanning into flames the heat that slumbered there.

His kiss deepened and his tongue flicked against hers as he caught her body in his strong hands and brought her towards him. His hands swept under the t-shirt, onto her bare skin, until they were splayed over her back, pulling her even closer to him, before sliding down and around her bare bottom.

Desire ground deep inside her as she pressed closer to him. His hand pushed up and cupped her breast, his thumb sweeping over her tightening nipple, causing cascades of sensation to tear through her body. She wriggled against him, all thought forgotten as desire ripped through her body.

Suddenly he lifted his mouth from hers and turned her so she lay flat on her back on the bed, with him above her. For one shocked moment, she wondered what he was going to do. Then, still holding his body away from her, he pushed up her t-shirt, that had already ridden high, lowered his head and turned his skilful tongue to her breast.

She pushed the palm of her hands against the soft mattress, about to lever herself away from his insistent mouth, but the ache of desire sank lower until it deepened into a wet, pulsating warmth that make her forget everything except the sensations which flooded her.

His lips nipped and sucked lazily at her breast, each rasp of his tongue sending shooting sensations through her body. The inner tension grew, compounding and heating, as his hand trailed over her stomach, and curved over her sex. She thought she'd explode with the strength of her own bodily craving, as she pushed against his palm.

Then his mouth followed the path of his fingers and he moved further down the bed. She pushed her fingers through his golden hair, exploring his curls, his scalp, the shape of his head as he moved further still.

He looked up at her suddenly with eyes that blazed with a dark passion, before he gave his full attention to that part of her which craved it.

She pressed herself back on the bed as pure, white electricity shot through her and she surrendered to the shock of the powerful sensations that swept her body. Tension, absorbing and compelling, coiled and surged within, increasing, building, insistent. Heat flooded her body and her breathing came shorter, panting, out of control. She gripped his hair once more, holding him there, needing more. Suddenly she cried out as light exploded within and her body reeled with the spasms that shook it.

She flung her arms behind her, luxuriating in the wanton release of her body and of her mind. She lay still, trying to regain her breath as he moved back up her body, laying a trail of kisses on her stomach as he went.

"That was amazing," she whispered, as he looked up at her.

"Glad to be of service," he whispered huskily into her ear, before nipping it lightly, causing her gut to flip with excitement and the tension to slowly coil once more.

She groaned and slid her palms tightly around his shoulders, relishing the curves of the muscles and sinew, their tautness and texture, before slipping down, cupping his shoulder blades and smoothing down into the small of his back, under his shorts, and over his buttocks that clenched under her touch.

They locked eyes in the soft gray light and she knew then that she wanted more. She'd never experienced such an orgasm with Paul, she'd never felt so intimate emotionally as she did with this stranger. And she wanted to feel him completely, within her body.

She moved her hands over him, making it quite clear what she wanted but he clamped his hand on hers and pulled it away.

He rolled onto his side, his head resting on one hand as

he held her gaze, a smile playing on his lips as he caressed her. She tried to pull him back into position but he stayed put.

"Sorry, I can't."

Perplexed, Gemma simply stared at him. "Can't? What do you mean?" 'Can't' wasn't a word she'd come across before in connection with sex.

"I have no protection here."

"I don't *need* protecting!" Just the mention of the word "protection" made her angry, reminding her of the over-protective, claustrophobic world in which she was raised, and the stifling virtual imprisonment of living with Paul.

The anger made her bold and she reached down for that part of him that she wanted inside her and held it between her hands, watching him close his eyes with pleasure and roll onto his back. The intense desire his kiss had triggered insisted on release. Besides, that was what she'd come to New Zealand for, wasn't it? To shed the shackles of her former life, to do as she pleased. Well, at the moment, *this* certainly pleased her. Besides, her periods were as regular as clockwork and she was at her safest point in her cycle.

"I don't need protecting," she repeated. "I want you."

She knelt on the bed beside him and, watching intently, focused on arousing him to a point where he'd forget his reluctance. She wanted him, and she *would* have him. She wanted to make love in her new home, to a new man, and have a new life.

She watched his face intently as he closed his eyes and groaned with pleasure. His body trembled and she was suddenly conscious of her power, which turned her on even more. She wanted him inside her.

But first she'd have to make him overcome his inhibitions about protection.

His breathing quickened and she lifted herself up and straddled him, sensing his control weaken. She kissed him then, dominating his mouth with her tongue, flicking his lips with her tongue, penetrating and then withdrawing just as she teased him below.

He pushed her hair from her face and kissed her. "Gemma? Are you sure you're okay with this?"

"Definitely."

And she was. As Callum responded she knew she'd succeeded in getting her way. And, as they came together in a sensual coupling she knew she was beyond definite—she'd never before experienced lovemaking like it.

Afterwards, he pressed his forehead against hers and for a long moment they were silent, neither moving, only their rapid breaths mingling, slowly calming, slowly returning to reality. Then he brushed her lips with his and rolled off, drawing her to him until her head rested against his chest.

"Gemma, that shouldn't have happened."

"Well, it did, and it's fine. And I, for one, am very glad. Aren't you?"

"Woman, you are seriously gorgeous. But I don't go around having unprotected sex."

She felt an unexpected flash of jealousy at the thought of this man having sex with anyone other than herself, protected or otherwise. But, more than that, she felt, for the first time she could remember, that she was where she was meant to be.

"I told you, I don't need protecting."

Her words seemed to reassure him. Her fingers trailed over his lips, so knowing and passionate, over the roughened stubble of his chin and his cheekbones, broad and strong. She traced his brows, darker than his hair, which framed eyes that were a smoky blue in the dull light. She touched his hair, then thrust her fingers into it and pulled him to her. She felt alive for the first time in forever as his weight moved on top of her and his mouth was hot against her skin.

He groaned as she curled first one leg around his hips and then the other, drawing her into him, claiming him as her lover. She felt her sexual power over him and reveled in it. But only for one moment before he growled her name, pulled her hands upwards, trapped them under his and she knew it would be on his terms after all.

Callum sat and watched Gemma as she slept, unselfconscious, draped across the bed. Her red hair, spread over the pillow like sunset over a cloud, her limbs slim and pale in the dull pewter light of early morning. Her chest rose and fell under the tangled duvet and his gut tightened with desire. Just the smell of her, the memory of the taste of her, aroused him. For all her initial shyness she was as wild as the mountains. She was a contradiction. But one he wanted to understand.

Since Claire had died, he'd avoided women. Claire had been his only love and he'd failed her. That was ten years ago. He'd never trust himself with love again. His family was hounding him to get over it and re-marry. But he was done with love. Since Claire, his relationships had been strictly practical. His only interest was the land, making the estate whole once more, and having heirs he could leave it to.

And this beautiful stranger, who'd come from nowhere, could deliver both to him. He went over and lay down beside her once more, kissing her shoulder gently so she wouldn't awake. Perhaps another marriage wouldn't be such a terrible thing after all.

## CHAPTER THREE

B y the time they both awoke, the sun's bright glare shone, unhindered, through the now un-shuttered window. Gemma carefully extricated herself from Callum's sleeping embrace and eased herself out of bed into the cool morning air. She opened the fire and dropped in a couple of the smaller logs whose loose bark sparked in the hot embers. She carefully replaced the lid, grabbed the towel that had dried overnight and made for the shower.

She stood in the bath, unmoving, under the blast of warm water, as she tried to come to terms with what she'd done. She twisted to allow the water to run across her breasts and stomach. Was it the whisky? She shook her head as she soaped her deliciously aching body. No, it wasn't that. Then what on earth had made her act so rashly?

She closed her eyes and the image of his eyes, darkened with lust, his muscles tense as he made love to her, filled her mind. It wasn't the whisky, it wasn't the jet lag, it was *him*. The water might rinse away the signs of their lust but not her memories of it. *They* would be forever burned deep within.

But it would make no difference. She'd come to New Zealand to find her freedom and she couldn't turn her back on that. It had been too hard-won. She tilted her head back and let the hot water sluice through her hair.

She re-entered the room and paused when she caught sight of Callum, dressed only in jeans, standing in the open doorway. She drew a sharp intake of breath as she was once more struck by his sheer strength and size. He was like a god, his strong profile and jaw thoughtful as he surveyed the trees that rustled in the brisk wind, the wide sunlit plains and clear, snow-capped mountain peaks. The bright sun highlighted the gold streaks in his hair, gold curls her fingers had found and twisted in the night as he'd brought her to orgasm. But now, standing there, she also felt the distance between them. She didn't know a thing about him. He was a stranger—an intimate stranger.

He observed her silently for a few moments. She swallowed, wondering what he was thinking. His eyes gave nothing away. "The storm's blown itself out. We should be able to cross the river."

A strange mix of disappointment and relief filled her. Of course they couldn't stay where they were forever, in this unreal world where everything was left behind. Life went on; life had just caught up with them.

"Great."

He looked at her carefully. Her inability to hide what she was thinking was obviously alive and well. "Everything okay?"

"Of course. Time to move on." She smiled and shrugged as she wondered what on earth would happen next. "I need to track down the car, salvage what I can from the wreckage, get myself a job and—"

"I'll get that sorted for you. Don't worry about it."

A spark of some familiar dread leaped up inside her, coming from nowhere. "That's kind of you but—"

"Don't worry about it. It's done. I'll get someone onto it."

An image of Paul slammed into her mind. One click of Paul's fingers would have men—and women—running to him. She looked away and tried to breathe deeply to calm herself. Callum wasn't Paul. She could leave at any time. He was just trying to help her out and she needed all the help she could get. "Okay, thanks. I'd appreciate it. I don't know my way around and I need to get to Blackrock, find my house."

"Blackrock?" He shook his head as if confused. "No, you may want to live in it at some point but until you've carried out basic repairs you can't stay there. You're coming back with me."

The wide, open expanse of the plains began to close in on her. "I'm what?" Her voice was soft with incredulity. Had she just spent the night with another control freak?

He huffed and held out his hands as if in appeasement. "I'm sorry, that sounded weird. I guess I'd imagined you'd be coming back with me, seeing as how Blackrock needs so much work. Seeing as how we've just spent the night making love, I assumed you'd want to."

She shook her head. "You assumed wrong. I have things to sort out."

"What things?"

"Everything—job, car, et cetera, et cetera."

"You can do all those things from home."

She bit her lip, uncertain, and stepped forward. "If you

think you need to do this because of last night, then don't." She took a deep breath. "I'm not under any illusion that it meant anything," she added, determined to give herself what she needed and give him what she thought he wanted to hear.

The light, that had before seemed too bright on Callum's face, suddenly darkened. He walked across to her until she was forced to look up at him.

"Didn't mean anything? I don't believe you." He reached out and pushed a wet strand of hair away from her face. It might have been that simple gesture or it might have been the unguarded look of tenderness in his eyes as he did it. Whatever, suddenly the fear of control left her.

"Of course it meant something. But you've got your life and I've got to sort one out for me. I didn't want you to think..."

He frowned. "I admit it was a strange way to meet someone. But that's what's happened and I want to see you again. And, as you are temporarily homeless, how about you come back to my house for a few days? Just," he added noting her hesitation, "until you get yourself sorted out."

She slipped her arms around his waist. "Well, Mr. Mackenzie, since you put it like that, how can I refuse?"

She pressed herself close against his naked stomach and chest, her fingers skimming over the ridges and hollows of his muscles as his lips took hers in a persuasive, and far too seductive, kiss. Her breasts were pressed hard against his body and absorbed the increased thudding beat of his heart, a beat mirrored by her own arousal. As his tongue explored her mouth, his hands deftly tossed away the towel and she was left naked. With a backward kick, Callum slammed the door closed and picked her up. She slid her legs around his waist and he walked across to the bed where he laid her down, stood back and undid his fly.

By the time they left the cottage, the sun was at its height and the white of the snow-covered mountains was brilliant against the bright blue sky. Looking around the high country now, it was as if there had never been a storm. The air was fresh and sweet and the golden plains spread before them with a grandeur and simplicity that seemed unchanging. But it did change. Its mood could swing violently from expansive and magical to restrictive and despotic in a heartbeat. The thought of the land's unpredictable nature caused the same tremor of concern she'd felt when Callum had announced she'd be going home with him. The concern grew slowly into an idea that refused to go away. Was she trading one sort of imprisonment for another?

Despite her underlying fears Gemma couldn't help being overwhelmed by the beauty of the rolling hills leading up to the mountains that towered in the distance.

"What's the name of the highest mountain over there?"

"Aoraki, Mount Cook—highest mountain in New Zealand. Didn't you read any guidebooks before you came?"

"No, no time." That was an understatement. She didn't know she was coming to New Zealand until a week before, when her friend had unexpectedly come up with a solution to her problem of where to run to. "I *do* know that it's part of a range called the Southern Alps. Schoolgirl geography."

"Not exactly impressive knowledge, considering your family came from here. Anything else? What's the name of this whole area, any idea?"

She shrugged. "Christchurch county?"

He groaned. "Nowhere close. It's the Mackenzie basin, Mackenzie country."

She shot him a quick look. "That's your name."

"There are plenty of us with Scottish names out here."

She relaxed once more. She didn't want to be with any big time property baron. All she wanted was a low-key life, lived under the radar, so Paul could never find her. Couldn't get much more low-key than a shepherd, she thought to herself.

"Anyway, how come we're heading towards the mountains? I thought we'd return the way we came."

"The bridge's gone and the river's too deep there. There's a crossing just north of here which should be passable now."

She certainly hoped so because, as they approached the river, it still appeared swollen and dangerous to her eyes. But Callum drove slowly through the wide river that rose alarmingly all around them. After much bumping and revving over the stony riverbed, they emerged on the other side and climbed the far bank, passing the high water mark, which was littered with branches and debris. It would have been impassable at that level. Once again, Gemma thanked her lucky stars Callum had come by when he had.

They drove on towards the hills, overshadowed by the Southern Alps and entered a valley high above the surrounding plains, Gemma noticed the land wasn't so wild. Fences and small houses dotted the landscape. She sat forward and blinked her eyes in surprise as she peered into the distance.

Framed by tall trees behind, and a smooth lake that acted like a mirror in front, was a sprawling two-story nineteenth-century mansion, complete with not one but two ivy-covered towers that flanked the porticoed entrance.

"Wow! What's that?"

"Glencoe."

"It's huge." They drove around the lake, up an avenue of lime trees, their vivid green leaves flashing bright in the late sun. Around the house were dotted buildings, houses, farm offices. It was like a small village. "You work here?"

He glanced at her. "Yes."

"Pretty amazing house. Are its owners as snobby as the house looks?"

"Some of them."

"Oh well. I guess it's worth putting up with people like that to live in this place. It's beautiful."

"Yes, my thoughts exactly."

She looked around. The houses where, no doubt, the workers lived appeared well kept and comfortable, if a little small. "Which house do you live in?"

Callum swung the car around the top of the drive and pulled up beside the front door which was as imposing as the rest of the house with its pillars and wide steps down to the drive.

"This one." He pulled on the handbrake, cut the engine and grinned. "Glencoe."

"But..." She frowned. "Don't they mind? Having the workers stay in the house?"

His gaze drifted to her hair, which he pushed back while stroking his thumb down the side of her cheek. "They've made an exception in my case."

"Really?" She grinned back, teasing. "Because you're so tall and strong and handsome?"

"That, and because I own the place."

Her grin fell from her face as shock and dread filled its place. "No, you're a shepherd."

"Only when I want to be." He swept his hand over her

now frowning face and kissed her briefly on the lips. "Come on. I'll show you around."

She watched him get out the car and greet a man who emerged from the stables. She didn't move for a moment, just watched him. One minute she felt she knew him, she trusted him, was safe with him. And then something like this. She'd got him wrong. What else had she got wrong? Only one way to find out.

"Morgan, this is Gemma. She's come to stay for a while."

Gemma slammed the car door closed and walked up to them and shook Morgan's hand. She wondered whether there was something in the water at Glencoe that made all the men so tall and fit. Callum put a protective arm around Gemma. "Morgan's my right-hand man." Gemma noticed Morgan's expression didn't change.

"Nice to meet you, Morgan."

"And you." He took a couple of steps back as if he couldn't wait to get away. "If you need anything, just give me a shout."

As Morgan returned to the stables, which were set back to one side of the house, Callum collected Gemma's bag and put his arm around her and walked up to the front door.

"Is Morgan related to you or do all Glencoe men look alike?"

Callum laughed. "No, we're not related. He hasn't been with us long but he's already made himself pretty invaluable." He opened the front door and held it open for her. "Welcome to Glencoe."

She stepped into a large room and turned 360 degrees, taking in the portraits that lined the opulently wallpapered walls, the ornate, Adam-style fireplace around which sofas were grouped and the rich reds and blues of the fine oversized rug on the polished floorboards. A two-story wooden staircase with a gallery at the top swept up at the rear of the space.

"Wow! Those paintings, are they all your family?"

"Apparently."

"Amazing place." Gemma had seen luxurious homes in England—had lived in one with Paul—but nothing like this. It was as if she'd walked back in time. "So, do you live here, in this huge house, alone?"

"Mostly. Family comes and goes—my mother, brothers and my elder brother's family. But otherwise I'm on my own. I have people who help around the house and the farm, but at night I'm alone."

"So, no wife then." She caught his eye and smiled. "That's good."

But he didn't smile in response. "I had a wife. She died."

"I'm so sorry."

He shrugged. "So was I—but that was a while ago now."

"So, have you always lived here?'

"Yep. My great, great grandfather built it—Caleb Mackenzie. He emigrated from Scotland in 1870, bought up all the land hereabouts and built this house."

"You still own all this land?"

"Not all of it." His voice had dulled suddenly. "But I will."

She looked at him sharply, trying to discern the meaning behind the edge to his words. But before she could say anything further, he'd moved on.

"Come on, I'll show you around."

Callum showed her through reception rooms, designed to impress, through to the rear of the property, which was obviously where he spent most of his time. The rooms were still on a large scale, but the furnishings were more comfortable, less lavish.

"I've never seen anything like this place."

"My ancestor did things on a grand scale."

Gemma wandered over to the French windows. As opposed to the formality of the front of the house, the garden at the back was designed in a natural style, with paths disappearing into woodland.

He dropped her bag to the floor. "I'll have Maria take your bag upstairs for you." He turned around just as the door opened and a middle-aged woman appeared.

"Good morning Mr. Mackenzie. Morgan received your message and has sent people down for Miss Winters' car."

Gemma raised her eyebrows.

"Good, Maria, this is Gemma Winters. She'll be staying with us a while."

Would she? Something inside her sent a loud warning signal through her system.

"Certainly, sir. I'll have a room prepared."

"And we'll have something to eat now in the Orangerie." He glanced at Gemma, a wicked gleam sparking in his eyes, as he looked her briefly up and down. "A lot to eat."

As Maria left the room, Callum's cell phone rang and she watched him stride over to the window, his gaze focused on the mid-distance as he concentrated on the phone call. He was so obviously lord and master of all he surveyed. How could she have thought otherwise? A cowboy? A shepherd? How could she have been so stupid? Here, back in the real world, he was a wealthy businessman—same toys, same arrogant commands over the phone. What the hell had she agreed to? She checked where her bag was and backed away from him. She'd get a taxi and return to civilization.

He looked up, switched off his phone and stared at her.

"You look as if you've seen a ghost."

"I think maybe I have."

He was beside her immediately. "I know this has all happened quickly, but I want you to stay."

"But—"

He stopped her words with a kiss, so gentle that it stunned her more than anything else he could have done. More than the passion they'd shared, more than any words he could have uttered.

"Stay, at least for something to eat. Then decide. Besides, it'll give my people a chance to locate your car."

She wondered if she'd be able to get a taxi to come all this way, even if she could afford it. "I'll get another rental." She winced, suddenly realizing that her finances weren't up to paying for another car.

"No." He sighed. "You can use one of ours if you need to. Look. Just have something to eat while we sort out a car for you."

She nodded jerkily. "Okay, thanks."

He placed his hand in the small of her back and ushered her into the Orangerie that ran the length of the rear of the house. The large exotic plants created screens and separate hidden areas. In the center was a table and chairs beside a small fountain.

"Geez, things don't seem to have changed here since the Victorian times."

"I hardly notice it. I leave the inside up to mother. She lives in Christchurch but visits regularly and what she says goes for the interior. I have no interest in it."

"It's beautiful. What was it like growing up here?"

Callum's gaze narrowed as he looked out to the trees that rose sharply behind the house. "Difficult. My parents didn't get on. How about you? Where did you grow up?"

"London. My upbringing was difficult, too, but for different reasons. My mother left my father and me when I was a baby. My father traveled a lot so we didn't see much of each other. I was really raised by my nanny. Then my father died and everything changed. It turned out he'd spent all the money."

"How old were you?"

"Seventeen."

"And you had no one you could turn to?"

"No, not at first. I did waitressing for a while and then... well..."

"And then when the old lady died, you came here."

Gemma started to deny it but bit her lip and nodded.

"What relation exactly was she to you?"

Gemma hesitated. "Distant cousin."

"When she died, you inherited Blackrock."

"I came to Blackrock, that's right."

"But your name's different."

"Er, yes." Damn right it was. "It came to me through my grandmother who married a Winters." Gemma looked at him anxiously, but the slight tension, the frown, disappeared as he obviously rationalized it to himself. "Right. So why did you come here?"

A thousand thoughts ran through her mind but she was saved by the entrance of Maria and the delicious smell of a homemade soup and fresh bread.


"Better?"

Gemma sat back. "Much, thank you."

His phone rang. Callum put it to his ear, listened, but barely spoke before switching it off once more.

"Any news on the car?"

"They've found it."

"Can it be saved?"

"Don't worry about it. I'll sort it out."

"And it's okay to borrow a car to take me to Blackrock?"

He frowned as his phone rang again. He glanced at the screen. "I have to take this call."

She rose, picked up her bag and stood by the open door looking out at the huge landscape. The longer she delayed, the more her resolve faltered. Eventually he finished his phone call and came over to her.

He lifted her chin and kissed her gently, persuasively.

"I want you to stay, Gemma. You don't belong in a rotting house in the middle of nowhere in the Mackenzie country. You wouldn't last two minutes. Stay here with me." Gemma didn't know whether he was talking about an overnight stay or something more permanent. And, from the frown that lingered on his forehead, he wasn't so sure himself. Either way she wasn't interested, no matter how much his kisses threatened to destroy her resolve.

"No, I have to go."

He frowned. "And where are you going to go?"

"Blackrock." She turned around, looking every which way but at him, and pushed her hands through her hair in confusion. "Just... got to go. I'm sorry, it's hard to explain."

Suddenly, he brought his mouth to hers once more and the kiss deepened as his hands slipped around her hips and bottom, drawing her closer still to him. The seconds extended into minutes during which Gemma's fears seemed to float away on a cloud of sensuous exploration of tongues and hands. With their bodies pressed so close together she was in danger of forgetting her own name.

Eventually he pulled away. "You're not going alone."

A cold shiver ran down her spine. Suddenly she remembered her name. Suddenly she remembered why she was here. Suddenly she remembered everything—too vividly. They were the exact same words Paul had spoken to her as she'd left him. She closed her eyes in disbelief at her stupidity. She was drifting into a relationship with another controlling man.

She pulled herself away from his arms. "Yes, I am."

He searched her eyes as if trying to make sense of her refusal. "Come on, you don't know your way there. I'm simply offering a lift, no strings attached—just a lift to Blackrock."

And she needed one. Because she'd got herself stuck in the middle of nowhere with a stranger and she needed his help to get to her new home. She sucked in a deep breath. "Okay. Thanks."

He frowned. He didn't have a clue what was going through her mind and she couldn't tell him. She couldn't tell him anything of her fears. She couldn't talk about Paul, couldn't mention she'd lied to him about being heiress of Blackrock. If there was one thing she'd learned in life, it was that a secret is best kept if you tell as few people as possible. Certainly not a stranger.

"I don't know what's going on, Gemma. You seem scared. Can't you tell me?"

She bit her lip and shook her head, willing her eyes to convey to him the words her mouth couldn't speak.

"Okay." He dropped her hands abruptly. "We'd better get going then. I'll take you to Blackrock and you can see for yourself what you're getting into."

She could see how she'd missed it. The small copse of trees hid its treasure well. As they ascended the overgrown track —indistinguishable from the surrounding tussock grass—the trees thinned and Gemma caught sight of a picturesque colonial cottage peeping out from behind a stand of huge pine trees.

She'd never considered the expression "love at first sight" as something real. But that's exactly what she felt now, for that lost house. She also felt a stab of regret because it wasn't actually hers.

"It's beautiful."

"It's a wreck."

She got out the car and walked up to the old verandah. She pulled at a piece of dead wisteria and tossed it onto the overgrown garden. "Nothing a bit of hard work won't remedy."

"You can't be serious, Gemma. It hasn't been lived in for years. The old lady who used to live here has been in a nursing home for nearly twenty years. And it was practically derelict when she was here."

She pulled out a key from her bag. "Just as well I put the key in my bag, and not the car."

"You stopped off at the lawyers first then."

"Yeah." She didn't want to talk about that. She'd given the lawyers Sarah's letter with the instructions that Gemma would be staying there indefinitely and to give her every assistance. The lawyers had been curious but hadn't quizzed her.

She pushed open the door and went inside. The too-long-closed-up smell of dusty emptiness filled her lungs.

The floorboards creaked and groaned as they stepped onto them.

"At least no one could come in here without you knowing." Callum raised his eyebrows. A shiver ran down her spine. "Seen enough to convince you this is a bad idea yet?"

"No." She walked through the hall, opening doors as she went. The rooms were large. It was nothing on the scale of Glencoe but the rooms had high studs and good proportions. But he was right. It needed a lot of work. But something had happened as she'd walked into the house. She'd felt an overwhelming sense of relief. It was a wreck. But, to all intents and purposes, it was *her* wreck. She turned around to find Callum standing close. He reached out and gripped her hands firmly within his. She shivered, both from the memory of what they'd experienced during the night and at his sense of possession as he held her hands tight.

"You have nothing here. No bed, no furnishings, no power."

"I'll manage."

"Well, there's some kerosene in the garage to fuel your oil lamps. But be careful about fire." He sighed. "At least you have water from the water tank." He shook his head in disbelief. "How are you going to cope, Gemma? You're hardly a country girl. Just tell me why you want to stay?"

"Instinct. It feels right here. It's what I've come to New Zealand for. To be free of things."

"Things? Like me, like men you mean? Perhaps you should have thought of that before we made love."

"I tried. Believe me I tried. But it was something..."

"Special. Wasn't it?"

She nodded. "But it's not what I came here for." She bit her lip. She had to tell him something of the truth. She owed him that. "I need to be free." She looked down at his hands that still gripped her tightly. "You make me feel trapped, controlled." He followed her gaze and slowly released his fingers. He stepped away.

"I don't mean to." He shrugged. "It's who I am. I'm in charge of the estate, I own it, I control it. It's who I need to be."

"You don't need to control me. I don't want you to."

"So I'm just meant to let you go and make a huge mistake?" He shook his head. "I don't think so."

They stared at each other in an impasse that she knew went deeper than words.

"It's my land, Callum, and I'm going to live here." He still didn't look as if he'd got the message. What the hell could she say to make him see? "Callum! I don't need you!"

It worked. Something like the shock of recognition passed over his features. He looked at her with a brief bewilderment that nearly undid her. She flexed her hands to stop herself from reaching out to him.

He stepped away. "Perhaps I was wrong. I thought you'd fit in. I thought you were different. But you're not, are you? You're just like all the rest."

She shook her head wondering what the hell he was talking about, but his sudden coldness took her breath away, robbing her of speech.

"Morgan will drop off a car to you later today," Callum continued. "Tell him if you need anything, because it's obvious you're not going to tell me."

She nodded. "Thanks." She followed him out into the bright sunshine, blinking lightly as if awaking from a sleep.

As she watched Callum drive away, out towards the hills, framed by the vast snow-capped mountains and rolling plains, she felt desperately sad. For a brief time she'd thought she'd found something she'd dreamed of her whole life through—a soul mate. But the dream had twisted into the old nightmare of possession and ownership. If Callum now believed her to be like every other woman, she believed him to be too like Paul for comfort.

She turned away abruptly and gazed up at the decrepit homestead. She could deal with sadness. So long as she had her freedom, she could deal with anything.

## CHAPTER FOUR

*Five months later...*

Gemma pulled up in front of the house, switched off the car engine and waited for the dust and quiet to settle. It was mid-summer and, although patches of rusting iron still peppered the roof and the weatherboards were in dire need of repainting, the house looked like home. There was an old sofa on the shady verandah and the blowsy white blooms of a climbing rose, uncovered after a ruthless attack on the overgrown garden, dangled heavily over the verandah, their petals covering the deck and garden like snow. She might not own the house, but, after a long shift at The Lakehouse Café in Shelter Springs, it was both home and haven to her.

Particularly now she'd discovered she was pregnant.

It had been a total shock when the pregnancy had been confirmed by the over-the-counter test. She'd managed to ignore all the signs, fooled herself into believing that her one slip-up had had no lasting consequences. But not any more.

Now the signs were all too obvious. She was five months pregnant and showing.

She slammed shut the car door and felt the full force of the mid-afternoon sun on her head. Once inside she walked through the dark hallway to the rear of the house where sunshine streamed into the kitchen and dining room.

She dropped the paper bag of groceries onto the kitchen counter, and plucked a postcard from her handbag and tapped it thoughtfully against the worn Formica. All the time she'd been here she hadn't received any mail. And now this. A post-card from London, with no words, nothing except her name and the name of the café. Was it Paul? Had he somehow found her? She couldn't believe it. It wasn't his style. He'd be over here on the next plane if he knew where she was. No, it must be Sarah, keeping in touch. She'd told Sarah she'd intended working in a café and there weren't that many to choose from so she must have hazarded a guess. But why didn't she send it to the house? Why no message? She sighed and propped the card up on the plate rack. She had no idea and no way of finding out. She couldn't risk writing to Sarah. Particularly now she had more to think about than herself.

She made herself a cup of herbal tea and walked into the dining room. The scent of lavender filled the air from the huge bunch of clippings she'd gathered together in an old tin fish kettle she'd found in one of the outbuildings. It was a large, high-ceilinged room simply furnished—by necessity—with a rickety table liberated from the curbside, a speaker system for her iPod and an old deckchair positioned in front of the French windows that looked out to the mountains.

But what dominated the room were the paintings. They were huge, rough canvases made of whatever she could find or afford, with sweeping wide brushstrokes courtesy of the paintbrushes she'd discovered amongst the century-old clutter in the shed. She wasn't happy with any of them but each of them expressed something of the sense of peace and freedom she'd found here, in this house, in Shelter Springs.

She switched on her iPod and the haunting strings of Vaughan Williams' *Thomas Tallis* filled the air. She turned the volume up higher, sipped her tea and stood looking critically at the painting she was currently working on. She picked up the brush and soon became absorbed in putting paint to canvas, creating order from chaos.

Time must have slipped past because her tea was cold as she sipped it and the sun had dropped lower in the sky, its beams enriching the unvarnished wood floor and cheap watercolor paints she was using. She stood still for a moment as she tried to think what had disturbed her. She turned down the music and stood motionless, listening. Then she heard it again—the creak and crack of the floor-boards as it came into contact with heavy feet. Fear sliced into her gut and she spun around.

It was Callum. He stood before her, just as she'd imagined him so many times, his hair as golden as the sun-bleached grasses that covered the valley floor and his body, tall and broad, bigger than she remembered. And she remembered often. The fear fractured and transformed into butterflies.

"What are *you* doing here?" She wiped the paint off her brush and stood tall, making sure to hide her stomach.

"I knocked but there was no reply. Your music was too loud."

"I wasn't expecting anyone."

"No." Long seconds passed while he stood looking her

over. It was just as before, a frank appraisal during which she felt as if she were stripped naked. She had to stop him.

"Callum, why are you here?"

"I've come to see you."

She raised her eyebrows in brief surprise. "Come to discover how I could possibly manage in this, what did you call it, 'wreck of a home,' without you?"

"No. I've come to see *you*."

She watched as his eyes ranged over the tired and shabby furnishings, the rotting window frames, before settling on the things she didn't want him to see—the most private expressions of her innermost feelings and thoughts that no one had ever seen. Her paintings.

"Well, as you can see, I'm fine. So don't let me keep you. I'm sure you've more important things to do."

"No, I haven't." He walked around the room, stopping at each of the dozen or so large boards that she used in lieu of canvas. "These yours?"

"As you're no doubt aware, I have no money so I've hardly bought them. They're just abstracts, ideas, that's all." She felt exposed and unnerved as he looked at her, a sharp curiosity evident in his stare.

"They have a feel of the Mackenzie country. I didn't know you were an artist."

"Why should you? We were together less than twenty-four hours. You don't know me at all."

"Perhaps," he touched one of her drawings, "like your sketches, I know the lines of you, but not the detail."

His reply shot down the words of self-defense that were already forming in her mind and stirred the powerful physical reaction just being in his company had on her. She sucked in a deep breath. She couldn't be swayed by him. She had too much to lose–especially now.

"I'd keep your knowledge to the lines if I were you. You might not like the detail."

He didn't respond, but continued to walk around the paintings until he came to a stop in front of her. There was no flicker in his expression, no movement of his eyes. She could hardly meet his steady gaze that bored into her, as if he could tell all he needed to know by looking at her.

"You're well, Gemma?" She swallowed and nodded. "You look tired."

"A little. *You* don't though. You look..." She couldn't finish her sentence, couldn't tell him how utterly devastating he looked. He didn't just look well, he looked gorgeous. His tan had deepened under the summer sun and pale lines radiated out from his eyes, a result of squinting into the bright light, she assumed. He still had a day's worth of golden stubble on his face but it couldn't hide the strong line of his jaw, nor the absurdly sensuous line of his lips. She cleared her throat. "You look fine. Anyway if all you came here to do is tell me I look tired..."

"It's not." He paused. "Don't I get a drink?"

She shrugged. "Sure. Tea? Water? I'm afraid I don't have anything else."

"Water's fine, thanks."

It was a relief to go into the kitchen and pour him a glass of water. When she re-entered the dining room, he was looking at her paintings once more.

"You're good. Very good. Do you sell them?"

She passed him the water and felt an erotic charge flow between them as their fingers touched briefly.

"No, they're not good enough. I just do them for me."

"What else do you do, just for you?"

She frowned. "What do you mean?"

"No boyfriends?"

She shook her head. "No. Although I don't see that's anything to do with you."

He shrugged. "That depends."

She arched an eyebrow. "On what?"

"On whether your baby is mine or not."

She closed her eyes, shocked as much by the hard, low voice as by his words. "So you've heard."

"Of course. Did you think you'd be able to keep something like that a secret?"

"I had high hopes."

He kept his eyes focused on her. "You haven't answered my question. Is the baby mine?"

"Of course it is!" She flung down the paintbrush she'd been crushing in the palm of her hand and paced away from him. "What do you think? That I'd gone and had unprotected sex with someone else immediately afterwards?"

"I wanted to hear it from you." His gaze followed her restless pacing around the room. "I thought you were on the contraceptive pill. Otherwise I'd never have had sex."

She shook her head. "No. No pill. I thought I was in a safe point in my cycle. Hadn't taken into account how the jet lag and exhaustion would upset my body." She shook her head again, bitterly. "Stupid, so stupid."

"Yes, you were. But so was I. You'd said you didn't need protection and I'd believed you."

She glanced up at him as she remembered what she'd said. "That word—protection—had bad connotations for me. I didn't want to be protected from anything or anybody. I'd had enough of that."

"You need protection now. You can't bring up a child in this house. Alone, penniless..." He looked around the room without focusing on anything in particular. He was buying time, for what she didn't know. He turned to face her once more, his gaze now determined and fierce. "I have a proposition."

"I'm not interested in any prop—"

"Listen to me! You can keep your freedom but you come to Glencoe. You marry me." He held up his hand, stopping her from speaking. "You get to stay in New Zealand like I hear you still want to do, you get a father—a family—for the child and no money worries."

"And in return you get..."

"My child."

Gemma turned blindly to the painting and closed her eyes. A family for her child. It was what she'd never had. It was what she'd vowed she'd always give her children. She opened her eyes but still didn't turn to him, just focused on the wet paint that glowed in the rich evening light. "And I'd have my freedom, you say?"

"Yes."

"How would that work exactly?"

He walked over to the window, hands thrust into his jeans pockets, his eyes narrowing against the brightness. A shiver of lust sliced through her stomach at the sight of his body, muscles tight and sinuous, rimmed by the rich, red light.

"You can come and go as you like. I won't..." He paused although his expression didn't change. Whatever he was thinking, whatever he was feeling, he was keeping it well in check. "I won't make any demands on you."

She raised her eyebrows in surprise and nodded agitatedly. "Right. Of course."

"This is purely practical. I don't want a relationship."

Gemma's head throbbed with the tension of wanting what she shouldn't want. "No relationship," she repeated.

"No. No relationship, I want an arrangement."

"But why, Callum? Why bother at all? You obviously don't want to be with me, so why not leave me to my own devices?"

"Because I'd never leave my child to grow up in poverty. When my wife died, so did any thought of love. I'm not interested in that any more. I had it once and don't wish for it again. But I want a child to leave Glencoe to. Marry me, and I'll get what I want and you'll never have to worry about money again."

She was shaking her head before he'd finished his sentence. "Callum, no. It doesn't work like that. Listen to me."

"I'm listening."

"I can't do it. I just can't."

"Don't you want the best for our child?"

"Of course I do. And I can give him the best—alone."

"Like your father did? So bitter about your mother that he had no time for a relationship with you. Even if you did want that for our child, I certainly don't. He'll be raised properly."

"Leave my family out of this. That's my business." She gripped the windowsill and leaned against the wall, willing her shaky legs not to crumple beneath her. What if Callum decided to investigate her background? What if he found out she wasn't who she said she was?

"The moment you became pregnant, it became my business too."

She turned to face him. Her short life in the real world had taught her the importance of not backing down. But it took all of her hard-learned lessons to meet the chill of his gaze.

"So my family wasn't a great role model. It doesn't mean to say I can't be."

Gemma gritted her teeth and jutted out her jaw, desperate to stop her inner fears surfacing. Callum Mackenzie didn't need to know that she was scared, so scared she wouldn't be enough for her child.

"I know you have courage, Gemma. But courage isn't enough to raise a child. And I want my child with me. There *will* be no other outcome."

"There has to be." She closed her eyes. She couldn't let him see the fear and pain she could no longer hide. His footsteps paced across the room as he huffed in frustration. He walked towards her again, she tensed and then he paced away again. She rubbed her aching temples back and forth as if to erase the conflicting emotions and confusion that raged inside.

She was aware of him standing behind her before he touched her. She sensed a shift in him before he spoke. His fingers raked the sides of her arms lightly but she couldn't move away. Instead she slowly opened her eyes as her body responded to the rightness of his touch.

"Tell me what it is you're so afraid of."

"Trying the soft approach now Callum? Not subtle are you?"

"You'll have your freedom."

"I can come and go as I please?"

"Within reason."

"Whose reason?"

"Mine of course."

She yanked her arm away. "You see, *this* is why it wouldn't work." She bit on her lip in an effort to stop herself moving back to him.

"So, tell me how it's working out, being on your own."

"I have a job."

"I told Lizzi to hire you."

His hands moved up her arms, his palms grazing the curves of her waist and shoulders, urging her to relax, to trust.

"I've got friends. A really good friend, Rebecca. She lives in Shelter Springs, works at the Observatory. I know she'll support me after I have the baby."

"It's not enough."

"And I have a car, a reliable car. Not the old bomb I bought after I moved in. So you see, I can look after myself."

"A job you won't be able to keep, friends, a car. Is that all you need to bring up a child?"

"And I've begun doing this place up."

"It's summer. What happens when winter comes? Our winters are fierce. It's often below freezing. How the hell are you going to manage then?"

"People managed years ago. I'll do the same."

"And this from the woman who can't even light a fire, can't make dinner."

"I can now. I've learned."

"I hope you haven't lit a fire here. I told you not to."

She frowned. "No, it's been too warm. And you had Morgan drop off the heater for me so there's been no need."

He sighed. "Anyway, it's beyond me why you left London in the first place. You'd have been more suited to living in a city."

"I wanted to be free to come and go as I wished, with no one stopping me. To live my life on my terms."

"And you couldn't do that in London? What or who was stopping you?"

She couldn't say a word. He'd come too close.

"Gemma! Who?" His frown deepened.

She shook her head. "I wanted wide open spaces. This," she gestured out the window, "is what I wanted." She looked out across the sun-streaked plains and listened to the tumbling of the river, the rustle of the ancient pine tree outside the window and the sweet tones of a skylark high overhead. "This is the sound of freedom now." She was listening to it. The soft murmurs of the Mackenzie country together with the knowledge that they were surrounded by hundreds of miles of empty landscape quieted and settled her like nothing else could. She took a deep breath. "And I'm determined to keep it," she added.

"You can have it at Glencoe. I won't demand anything of you—just that you be a mother to our child. You surely don't want to inflict a childhood like your own on our child? Only in your case you'll be poor as well—your only asset, a decaying house in the middle of nowhere."

The final twist of the knife. She spun around to face him, his eyes, colorless with his back to the light, were fixed on hers.

"And if I don't agree?"

"Let's not go there." He began to turn away but she put her hand on his arm.

"Yes, let's. I want to know where we stand."

"If you don't agree, I play dirty."

"I don't believe you play anything else." He'd moved in front of her and she searched his face before settling on his mouth. "From the moment you picked me up in your arms and threw me into your car"—she flicked her tongue around her lips to moisten them—"to when I awoke in the morning light to find your arm around me, your breath warm on my face."

Gemma could have sworn she heard both their hearts thudding in the quiet that descended as they both remembered with vivid clarity the passions of that night.

He traced his finger down her cheek before slipping one

long strand of hair between his thumb and forefinger and dragging it down straight, his finger grazing her breast. "Playing dirty? That was me playing fair. I saved you from being swept away by the river, remember? It was you who wanted sex."

"Tell me, Callum, what was it you thought then?" She couldn't help the bitterness creeping into her tone, a useful check to the heat and need that was building and coiling within at the onslaught of almost tangible memories.

"I had no thoughts that night—only needs."

"And that's the way you like it isn't it? Using each other for mutual pleasure and then? Nothing. No thoughts, no feelings."

"Why would that matter to you? Just think of your past, Gemma. Do you really want our child brought up by a solo parent, isolated, deprived, just as you yourself were?"

"I was deprived of love. My child won't be."

"You can't exist on love alone. Don't be ridiculous. You're so naïve."

"And you're so callous."

"Practical."

"Callous," she repeated. "And cold and everything I don't want near my child."

She felt the heat of his breath against her mouth. Somehow they'd moved closer to each other. How, she had no idea. She looked up into his face, her eyes drinking in the spark of heat she saw flickering in his eyes. For once she was out of words.

"I want my child, Gemma. And I will have him—with or without you. Which is it to be?"

She shook her head. "I can't believe I've come all this way to be deprived of the thing I wanted most—freedom."

"Is it what you want most now?"

Slowly she shook her head. "You know it isn't. It's my child's security and happiness."

"*Our* child." The words were breathed so that she barely heard them. "You *will* marry me."

Cold words from a heart that held no warmth. She looked out at the indigo sky seeking reassurance, inspiration, something, *anything* that would give her the strength to stay here alone. But there was none. Only a beautiful place that, with the change of seasons and no money, would become impossible to live in. She forced a smile to her lips.

"And, these terms, I can come and go, be as free as I like within this loveless marriage?"

He frowned. "Providing it doesn't reflect badly on the family, on me. Providing it doesn't affect our child." He cleared his throat. "No affairs, of course."

"Of course." She said sarcastically. "And no affairs for you, as well, I take it?"

"We'll work out the details later. Bottom line, you come to Glencoe and we raise our child together. This is all it's about. This is all that's important to me."

"And, to me..." Her hands came around her stomach—holding it, supporting it—as a deep sadness at what might have been swept through her. She'd tasted freedom. Yes, it had been freedom tainted by confusion and sadness after her night with Callum but, even so, she'd found a home here, out in the middle of nowhere, a life with friends in Shelter Springs. It could have been everything she'd been looking for. And it had transformed to dust before her eyes because of her own stupidity. She cleared her throat. "And, to me," she repeated stronger now. "My child is everything. I agree. We'll make a life together—God knows what sort of life—but we'll make one for the sake of our child. But, Callum?"

"Yes?"

"You must love him or her."

"Of *course* I will. He or she will be *my* child—a child I'll love and care for."

She nodded slowly, aware that, if nothing else, she could trust this big man to speak the truth. "Okay."

She hadn't realized until then how uncertain Callum must have been at her reaction to his proposal. It was only when she'd uttered her brief words of agreement that his face relaxed with relief. "Good. Pack your things—let's go."

She walked over to the French windows and tugged their warped frames sharply together in order to close them. They slammed shut and the glass rattled and the pane cracked. She gasped—the darkening sky looked as broken as the window.

"I'll get someone to fix it."

"No! Leave it." She turned away and had to bite her lip to hold back the tears. "I'll just put a bag of my things together. The rest—"

"I'll have someone pack it up and bring it over to Glencoe. We'll find a place for it somewhere."

"No, it stays here."

"But—"

"No, I don't want it moved. I want my paintings here. I want everything just as it is."

He was puzzled but she couldn't explain. She just knew that she couldn't sever her connection to this place so easily.

She walked into her sparsely furnished bedroom. It didn't take her long to pack a bag. Seemed she spent her life packing small bags and leaving. Difference was, this time she didn't want to go.

But, deep down, she'd known he'd show up some time. Their connection had been too intense to fade into nothing.

New Zealand was a small country and the Mackenzie country—of which his family owned a substantial part—was a small place within it. Through compulsion and circumstance she'd known their meeting was inevitable.

But of all the different scenarios that had played in her mind, one in which he appeared and coerced her into a loveless marriage, hadn't even entered her head.

# CHAPTER FIVE

H e must be mad. His household certainly thought he was. But if he was, so be it. There was no way he was leaving a child of his to be brought up in squalor. He'd have full control over his child this time. There were things he hadn't told Gemma about his wife, things that were nothing to do with her, but that had left an indelible mark on him. There was no way he was leaving a child of his to the vagaries of fate. He turned to see Gemma hesitating by her car.

"I'll follow in my car."

He sighed. "Get in."

"I can't just leave it there. It might get stolen." Her voice trailed off as she looked across at the late model BMW.

"I'll get someone to bring it over to Glencoe tomorrow." He paced up to her, grabbed her bags. "We'll go in mine."

"No, I'll go in my car."

He could tell by the jut of her jaw that he'd triggered her stubborn streak. Well, she'd met her match with him. "Gemma, just get in, will you? Or do I have to do what I did that first night? Pick you up and sling you over my shoulder?" He opened the door for her to enter.

Her eyes narrowed as they met his before she stepped into the car. He reached over grabbed the seat belt and strapped her in. Her face was like chalk, her brown eyes huge, but still she resisted.

"Trying to keep me restrained, Callum? It'll take more than a seat belt."

"It's for your own safety. And the baby's."

She swallowed, bit her lip and nodded stiffly as he closed the door on her. He jumped in beside her, switched on the ignition and roared away from her house, along the track towards Glencoe. Dust bloomed around them in the dying light of the long summer evening. Far in the distance the mountains rose, snow-capped and remote.

He'd been hard and he knew it. But he couldn't trust her not to turn around and head straight back to her homestead. And he wasn't about to let history repeat itself. This time *he* would be in control—for her and the baby's sake.

He glanced at her and saw she was staring at her house in the rearview mirror, watching it through the plume of dust in the darkening light. It had always been a landmark, one that had diminished over time as the trees had grown, but for some reason Callum couldn't fathom, Gemma's mark on the house had changed it.

She seemed to change everything she came into contact with. But he'd be damned if he'd let her change him. He was in control of his life. And that was the way it would stay. He wanted, he *needed* to care for his child. Period. There would be nothing else between him and Gemma. If he let his guard down he was afraid he'd let her into his life. He'd let his guard down once with a woman and he wouldn't be repeating that mistake.

No, once she was there, at Glencoe, he'd make sure she stayed. And he'd make just as sure he kept his distance.

The high mountains of the Southern Alps lay before them as they drove straight as an arrow up the river valley towards the Mackenzie land at Glencoe. Foothills, darkened and out of sight of the low sun, framed the massive plateau of the Mackenzie Basin. It usually had an uplifting effect on Gemma. But tonight the silence and long twilight of this southern land lay heavy on her heart, deepening her sense of loss.

"And why you had to drive me I don't know." She knew she was being petty. There was so much to say, so many important things and yet this was what rankled most at that moment.

There was no reply.

"It's not as if it was my old car. Now, that *was* unreliable." She sighed. It seemed she was talking to herself so she might as well continue. "No, I'm driving a BMW now. Surprised?" Not by his reaction, he wasn't. "Yes, I thought you might be. The mechanic couldn't repair my old bomb and said that I could use the BMW. The owner was a friend of his and was away for a while. Pretty generous really. So I've been totally safe driving around, in case you were concerned." She twisted in her seat to face him. "Somehow I don't think you were though, were you?"

"Gemma, you seem to have made up your mind about me, so I hardly think it's important what I say. Do you?"

She shrugged. "True. I rely on instinct to get me through life. It hasn't failed me yet." If only she'd believed her instinct when it shouted at her to not get involved with Paul. She glanced at Callum, his mouth and jaw, firm and grim. "I'm guessing instinct isn't something you're familiar with."

"My businesses take more than instinct to turn a profit."

"A computer can run a business. It can't run a life." Not her life anyway. Instinct had driven her to New Zealand, it had drawn her to the old homestead and she'd found a life for herself. And now it was gone again. It wasn't fair, but she'd always known life wasn't fair.

She was marrying a man who'd made it clear he had no feelings for her, for the sake of their child. It was a sacrifice that her parents hadn't been prepared to make for their child. And a lonely, love-deprived upbringing had resulted. She had no choice but to sacrifice her independence if she wanted to give her child a half-decent chance at life.

She fixed her gaze on Glencoe, the rich, red brick mansion standing apart from its dun-colored surroundings like the statement of might that it was. With its outbuildings, farmers cottages, estate offices and stables it looked like a world contained in itself—a medieval village where the Mackenzies were lord and master. The image seemed fitting somehow. She was to be married to a man who only wanted her for what she could bring to him—their child. Nothing much had changed in a millennium. It wasn't a cheering thought.

They drew up outside the sweep of steps that led to the portico that sheltered the front door. Their car doors slammed shut in the stillness of the evening and Callum opened the front door for her and stepped aside. "Welcome back to Glencoe."

She flicked up her eyes. "Ironic, since I feel I've been kidnapped."

"Don't be ridiculous. It's an arrangement that meets both our needs. That's all."

She entered the foyer ahead of Callum, her eyes adjusting to the darker interior. Nothing had changed since her last visit. She doubted anything had changed over the past century.

He looked at his watch. "Go and get changed. We're dining at eight."

She shook her head. "I'm not hungry."

"You *will* eat. And you *will* look after yourself. That's part of the deal."

"What are you going to do? Force feed me?"

"If I have to. But it won't be necessary because you *will* come to the dining room and you *will* eat." He looked over Gemma's shoulder.

Gemma turned to see the woman she'd met before, Maria. "Welcome back to Glencoe, Miss Winters. I've prepared a room for you."

Gemma frowned. "How did you know—"

"Any word from Lady Mackenzie?" Callum interrupted.

"Lady Mackenzie phoned, sir. She'll be joining you for dinner to meet Miss Winters."

Callum nodded. "Good. May as well get it over with."

Maria coughed. Callum turned to her. "And the BMW at Blackrock? Its warrant of fitness is overdue, I believe. Shall I have someone collect it?"

Gemma frowned and looked questioningly to Callum. "What—"

"Yes, please do, Maria." Callum placed a large hand on Gemma's back. "I'll show you to your room."

"I've prepared the guest room next to yours, as you requested." Maria said.

*Next to his!* Gemma contented herself with pushing

away his arm and giving him a glare until Maria had disappeared.

"Lady Mackenzie? How did she know I'd be here? Come to that, how did Maria know I'd be staying? And in the room next to yours?"

"I told them both. May as well face her sooner rather than later. This way, Gemma."

"And, while I'm at it, how does Maria know what kind of car I drive? Hmm? I met the woman briefly five months ago and she knows the model of my car and that its warrant of fitness is due. Explain that."

"You're not stupid, Gemma. Put two and two together."

"Oh, I have. And they've made twenty-two. You're the friend of my mechanic aren't you?"

"No, I'm not. But of course I arranged it for you. Your old car was completely unreliable. I didn't want you breaking down in the middle of nowhere."

"Why not? You'd jacked me up with the car way before even *I* knew I was pregnant. Were you paying me for services rendered? Or were you simply being kind? I don't believe you do anything for simple reasons, do you Callum?"

"You can read into it whatever you like."

"But, there again, I would never have known it was your car until Maria let the cat out of the bag. Payment for services rendered isn't usually anonymous. Kindness is though."

"Gemma, you're talking too much."

"Oh, am I? I didn't realize I needed permission from you to talk. Perhaps you'd be good enough to let me know when I should stop talking?"

"Any time soon would be good."

She contented herself with a glare at his broad back. They walked in silence along the mezzanine landing that ran the length of the hall below. The whole place glowed— the toffee-colored wooden rail, the gold and green ogee wallpaper and the gilt-edged landscape paintings that hung between the doors. He stopped abruptly.

"In here."

She walked past him onto the faded Turkish carpet of the simply furnished room. It was different, less elaborate than the others and didn't look out onto the formal view at the front of the house, but out to the back, to the woods and mountains beyond.

She folded her arms. "Nice view, nice room, but it's next to yours. Why? We've agreed we'd have no relationship. If I can't have my freedom on my own, I'm damn sure I'm going to keep it within our marriage. That's the deal."

"I can assure you I want nothing else from our marriage."

Gemma met his hard gaze. The sting in his words and cool tone of his voice hurt, as he'd intended. But they were a response to her own barbed comments. She couldn't seem to help it. If it wasn't for the constant hum of electricity that charged up as soon as he came close to her, she might have managed to be civil. But she found herself throwing hurtful words at him to stop herself from drawing close to the fire that smoldered between them. He could say whatever he liked, she could proclaim whatever she liked, but the reactions of their bodies didn't lie. "That's fine with me." Another lie. "I've surrendered my freedom to you. I'm not about to let you have my body too. We've made a deal. You get our child. You don't get me."

"So keep your end of the deal. Dinner tonight with

mother. Then, tomorrow, I've arranged a doctor's appointment for you. I expect you downstairs at nine."

"Fine!" she snapped back. "But don't think you can continue to order me around like this because I won't stand for it."

For a long moment they stared at each other as the anger and hurt raged inside her. She tried to see in his eyes some kind of chink in that hard surface, some kind of sign that he felt something more. There was no change, just a barely perceptible nod—its meaning ambiguous. A simple acknowledgement of her words or agreement? She didn't know.

She turned away and looked out the window. She closed her eyes as she heard him approach. He stood just behind her and her anger disappeared instantly, it was as if he'd put his arms around her and held her. Her body ached for his touch.

He cleared his throat. "The view's to the east—not the best, but I've always liked to see the sun rise."

"Me too. New beginnings." She bit her lip to stop it trembling. "Usually, they promise so much..."

He moved away without another word. The door opened and closed with quiet deliberation—just as he did everything else: with purpose, without fuss, with a finality that cut through to the bone.

She sat heavily onto the bed after he left and dropped her head in her hands. For all her bravado, she felt shattered.

*What had she done?* But she knew. It was the only thing that she could do to give her child the care that she'd been deprived of.

He couldn't take his eyes off her.

From the paintings that lined the room, her gaze flew to the furniture, to the food, to the books and then back to the paintings again, with a restless energy. If it was intelligence and curiosity that sparked in her eyes, it was sensuality that ruled her mouth.

She took a forkful of salmon, heaped with herb sauce and closed her eyes briefly, savoring the contrast between the piquancy of the sauce and richness of the fish. Her tongue flicked around full lips that were strongly defined and perfectly drawn.

His life had taken an unexpected turn but he was in control again now. More than that, he felt strangely relaxed, content even, simply watching her. She licked a tiny drop of glistening sauce from her lips. He remembered the taste of her on his lips and he involuntarily licked his own.

"You appear to enjoy your food, Miss Winters."

Inwardly Callum groaned as he glanced at his mother.

"I usually eat at The Lakehouse Café after my shift's finished. This makes a change."

"Café…" Lady Mackenzie echoed faintly.

"Yes, café. Eating there is one of the perks."

"One of the perks you'll no longer have, now you're not working there."

Callum noted his mother's smug smile with irritation.

Gemma frowned. "Of course I'll work there."

"No." Callum agreed with his mother on this point.

Gemma sat back, the cutlery landing on the plate with a clatter.

"No? Care to elaborate?"

"It's pretty obvious. You have no need to work in a café. And…" he shrugged, "you'll have your hands full soon enough."

"I see. So I have no say in this?"

He sat back, watching her, wondering why he had such a strong desire to goad her. Was it pleasure in seeing her so riled—her flushed cheeks certainly brought to mind another time when her skin had been glowing and her eyes bright—or was it some kind of retaliation against her, for so obviously not wanting to be here, with him?

"I spoke to the manager of the café this morning."

"You had no *right* to discuss my work with my boss. I'll keep on working if I want to."

"Miss Winters, if I may intercede on Callum's behalf, a café isn't a place for a Mackenzie woman."

Gemma looked from Callum to his mother, opened her mouth to speak before obviously thinking better of it. "Callum, we should discuss this later."

He shrugged. "Nothing to discuss."

"And *I* think there is. We'll talk about it later." She picked up her cutlery once more.

He sipped his drink. She'd find out soon enough that he'd only spoken briefly to Lizzi, the manager of the café. They were old friends and she'd rung him about something else. He'd only told her that Gemma would be in touch.

His mother appeared to have enjoyed the disagreement. "So tell me, Miss Winters, what do you intend to do with your new free time?"

Gemma shot her a dark look.

"Gemma's an artist, mother."

"Oh, really? What do you paint?"

Gemma took a deep breath. "Abstracts mainly. Not like the Woolaston over there." She nodded to a large canvas of rolling hills in subtle shades of green and ochre by one of New Zealand's most famous artists.

His mother laughed. "I should think not. *That* is a masterpiece. My late husband was a great collector. It's nice you have a hobby." She sipped her wine, paused and turned to Gemma again. It was obvious she wasn't going to let up.

"Gemma's a good artist, mother," interjected Callum, trying to pre-empt another shot at Gemma. "I've seen her paintings."

Gemma shook her head in denial. "I'm not very good, I just—"

"Art is such a subjective thing, wouldn't you say, Miss Winters?"

"Sure. Like just about everything else."

"Indeed. Sometimes it's hard to understand what someone is thinking of when they make big decisions, based on nothing more than"—she shrugged her elegantly narrow shoulders—"whim."

*First hit.*

His mother always managed to wind him up. She never came out and said exactly what she was thinking, merely insinuated, so she couldn't be opposed. It drove him mad. But he'd always found it best not to say anything at all. So he focused on his food and took another mouthful. When he looked up Gemma was glancing from him to his mother and back again.

"Anyway, Miss Winters—"

"Gemma, please."

His mother smiled a tight little smile that echoed the cool blue of her eyes. "I prefer not to assume intimacy after only minutes of meeting. Unlike others."

*Second hit.*

"I was wondering when the baby is due."

*Third hit.* It had come much sooner than Callum had

expected. He didn't know who was more surprised, Gemma or himself.

Gemma cleared her throat. "June."

"Oh," his mother said lightly. "So soon." She turned a cold face to Callum. "And the wedding, Callum, where do you intend to marry?"

He shrugged. "I hadn't thought about it."

Lady Mackenzie wiped her mouth on the napkin and placed it beside her plate with finality. "The Mackenzies have always married in Christchurch Cathedral. You married Claire there." She sighed. "But the cathedral is no longer, unfortunately. Thanks to the earthquake. I'll find somewhere else in Christchurch."

"How about somewhere closer to home?" He felt a pang of guilt when he saw how miserable Gemma looked. "What do you think, Gemma?"

She shrugged as if she didn't care. But she appeared to be diminishing under his mother's stony gaze. "Does it matter what I think?"

His mother's fine gray brow swept upwards. "Matter? My dear young lady, it *is* your wedding. I'd have thought it matters a great deal." She took a sip of white wine and placed the glass back on the mahogany table with deliberate care. "Claire organized her wedding most ably."

Gemma bit her lip and shook her head, fixing her eyes firmly on her plate.

"And I'm sure Gemma will organize our wedding most ably," Callum said firmly. "Especially if she's given some support." Callum was rewarded with a grateful glance from Gemma.

Lady Mackenzie shrugged noncommittally—a tense little shift of her narrow shoulders. "Our family weddings have always been in Christchurch. Even Dallas and...whatever her name is."

"Cassandra, mother. As you very well know, it's Cassandra."

Lady Mackenzie sighed. "American." There was a long pause. "Lovely children though." She faced Gemma once more. "I'll organize it for you. Leave you time to do whatever it is you want to do here." She waved her hand. "Paint, whatever you like. Leave the arrangements to me."

Gemma looked up at Callum, her eyes pleading.

"We might, mother. Then again, we might not. Gemma and I need to discuss things first—but not tonight."

His mother visibly stiffened and she sipped her wine delicately. "I see." She glanced down at her plate for a few moments before pinning Callum with a look. "Darling, I need my glasses. I think they're in the Orangerie. Would you be a dear and get them for me?"

Callum sighed. He knew it was a ruse. "I'll have Maria get them." Then he remembered he'd given Maria the evening off and there was no-one else close by. "Okay, I'll go." He shot his mother a warning look. "But I'll only be gone a few minutes."

"Thank you, darling." His mother's butter-wouldn't-melt-in-your-mouth look worried him more than any outright aggression. He shook his head in despair at his mother and left the room, determined to be as quick as possible.

Gemma watched Callum leave the room with a heavy heart. She felt exhausted and not up to playing cat and mouse with Lady Mackenzie. And a glance at Lady

Mackenzie's suddenly changed expression, only depressed her further.

"You're not right for Callum, you know. He needs someone of his own class, someone who can help him with the estate. Not someone like you. How much money do you want?"

"What?" Gemma couldn't believe the woman had the audacity to talk to her like that.

"How much money do you want to leave?"

Gemma shook her head, incredulous. "I'm not with Callum for money."

"What then?"

"It's about our child."

"If you think you'll be getting a father for your child from Callum, you're mistaken. He's focused on one thing only—his land. He'll have no time for you or the child. You've chosen the wrong man in Callum. You don't know him at all."

Anger at Lady Mackenzie's unjust comments both to her and Callum swept away her earlier intentions of saying as little as possible. Despite her personal grievances against Callum, the injustice of his mother's remarks—whether truly believed or simply designed to make Gemma leave—shocked her.

"I reckon I know Callum better than you do by the sounds of things."

"You know enough to get pregnant—that much is obvious."

"Enough to know that he'll do right by my—our—child. And," her voice lowered, "enough to know he's a good man."

Lady Mackenzie stared angrily into her eyes. "There's many a good man out there." She whirled her hand in the air. "Why don't you run along and find one more suited to you."

"I've found one. Callum will do just nicely thank you."

The heavy door swung closed behind them. In her anger she hadn't been aware that Callum had entered the room. Nor had Lady Mackenzie, if the flash of annoyance that passed over her face was anything to go by.

Lady Mackenzie rose at once, elegant and poised, but Gemma could see that Callum's entry was premature and unwelcome.

"Did you find them?"

"No, they weren't there. As well you know."

Callum was talking to his mother but his eyes were fixed on Gemma, searching her face as if looking for some kind of answer. What had he heard her say? His expression was uncharacteristically thoughtful.

"Gemma, are you okay? You look pale."

Gemma nodded. She wasn't the only one. Lady Mackenzie's face was drained of color as she looked from one to the other of them and Gemma could see she was even less happy than before. Lady Mackenzie took her seat once more.

"This is my business as much as yours, Callum. And I can see you're blinded by the girl. Just like a man. Just like your father." Her voice trembled as she looked away.

"Just stop right there, mother. My marriage is *my* business, no matter what you care to think. And I'd appreciate it if you stopped insulting Gemma and you didn't get involved in what doesn't concern you."

"Of course it concerns me." She glanced from one to the other and then back to Callum. "You don't even know the child is yours. Have you had a paternity test done?"

"Hang on a minute—"

Callum held up his hand to stop Gemma from rising from her seat. "I have no doubts that the baby's mine and this is none of your business."

"It most certainly *is* my business. I have a share in this land, if I may remind you, and this business."

"We are to be married next month and we're expecting the birth of our child in June. Those are the facts and you're just going to have to deal with them."

"So what are you getting out of this other than a bed-warmer and legitimizing a bastard?"

"None of your business."

She rose, walked towards him and coolly examined his face.

"But I think it is, isn't it Callum? It *is* business. There can be no other reason." Lady Mackenzie narrowed her eyes assessingly. "It's the land, isn't it? You've sorted something out about the land."

"It's time you left for home. It'll be dark soon and you know you don't like being driven in the dark."

She laughed and her face relaxed into a look of understanding that puzzled Gemma. "Well, well. A proper Faustian deal. Not so badly done after all, Callum." She walked up to him and kissed him on the cheek and left the room, closing the door behind her with an eerie softness. Gemma slumped back into her chair.

Callum strode across to the window and watched his mother impatiently await her car under the stone portico. It was only when the smooth purr of the Bentley moved away that he spoke.

"I must apologize for my mother. She's, well"—he shrugged—"upset, I guess."

"*She's* upset! There can be no excuse for her behavior. She's like some Valkyrie."

"Yeah, well. She had a rough life with my father, but... you're probably right. There's no excuse for saying the things she did." He paused, searching Gemma's face for what, she didn't know. "You look tired. You should go to bed."

She rose slowly. "Damn it, Callum. I'd appreciate it if you didn't tell me when to go to bed. I don't need to be told what to do, I don't need to be controlled. I'm not a child."

"I know."

His quiet admission cut through her anger and robbed her of speech.

He walked over to her until he was so close that if she'd reached out, she'd have been able to touch him. "I know you're not a child. But it doesn't stop me from wanting to make sure you do the right thing—from wanting to look after you." He cleared his throat. "It's a practical thing, you understand, not emotional. You mustn't expect anything like that from me."

She should have been inured to hurt by now, but apparently she wasn't. She drew a deep breath.

"Don't worry. My expectations are low on that score."

"So we have an understanding?"

"Yes. But it'll be easier to stick to it, if you and your mother stop throwing your first wife in my face. I get it that she was a paragon of virtue and I'm nowhere close, but I really don't need to hear it again and again."

"She wasn't."

Gemma waited for him to elaborate but he didn't. She sat back in her chair, puzzled. "Wasn't what?"

"A paragon of virtue."

"What do you mean?"

He looked outside once more. The house lights and those of the surrounding buildings formed a pool of brightness, around which the shadows of early twilight clung. "I'm not going to elaborate. Just wanted you to know you've nothing to live up to. I loved Claire but she had her problems, our life wasn't straightforward."

She hadn't thought it would hurt so much to hear that he loved Claire. "So how did you go from love to emotional shutdown?"

"Give it a break, Gemma. I lost her." He sucked in a difficult breath. "Okay. I'll tell you. She was headstrong—it was one of the things I loved about her—but it led her to do things she shouldn't. She was easily influenced. And I let her do what she wanted. I shouldn't have. She died because of it." The words were cold, clipped and business-like.

Instinctively Gemma reached out to comfort him. He stared intently at her hand resting lightly on his arm.

"Her death was my fault. And I fully intend to make sure that I don't make the same mistake again. I *will* take care of my own."

"Even if that means taking over someone's life, Callum?"

He shrugged. "Whatever's necessary."

"You can't take on everybody's issues. You need to give them—you need to give *me*—space."

"I need to keep you and our baby safe. That's the bottom line, that's the end of it." He turned away abruptly.

The conversation was at an end. It had shifted out of his comfort zone into the world of emotion. And yet instinct made her want to bridge the gap between them, to take him in her arms and hold him so tight that he *would* feel her. But he'd just made himself perfectly clear—he had no interest in her, other than keeping her safe.

She left the room without a glance and closed the door. She walked through the softly lit house to her room, feeling the hurt in every cell of her body. Yes, he was considerate, as someone is about someone, or something, in their care. He'd made sure she had a good car to keep her safe, he'd tried to stick up for her against his mother's verbal onslaught. But that was as far as it went.

She'd imagined he couldn't love, couldn't feel. But he did. Just not for her.

# CHAPTER SIX

D r. Cooper peered up at her over the half-rimmed glasses with a probing gaze.

"Keeping well?"

Another man of few words. What was it with these country men?

"Fine." She crossed her legs and folded her arms. At least few words would mean they'd get through this more quickly. She glanced at Callum who stood by the open window, looking out across the glass-like stillness of Shelter Lake, the mountains reflected in the pristine surface.

"Any conditions in the family we should take account of?"

"Like what?"

"Your mother's pregnancy ran smoothly?"

She shrugged. "No idea."

"Umm." The doctor examined his papers. "And why is that?"

"She didn't stay around long enough for me to find out."

"Your father?"

Gemma noticed that Callum's gaze had stopped

sweeping the water and he'd become still, just like the trees and lake outside the window, calm and expectant. He obviously wasn't as disinterested as he appeared.

She squared her shoulders. "Died. Look, doctor, I'm sure you mean well, but I'm fit, I've been working up until now. I'm just having a baby. Everything's fine, everything's normal."

The doctor's lips twitched, but there was no smile in his eyes. "I'm sure it is." He sifted through her non-existent file. "Now, where can we find your old medical records? There may be information in them we need."

She shrugged again. "London, I guess. I haven't seen a doctor since I left home."

"And when was that?"

She stood up, exasperated. No way was she going into her background with Callum standing by. "Thank you for your time, but I really don't need any of this."

"Miss Winters. You *are*, of course, free to leave at any time."

"No, she's not. She's sick. Look at her." Callum faced them for the first time, irritation showing through the usual impassive mask.

"A little anemic, I think. Not unusual with prolonged morning sickness. She'll be fine after a few months, with rest and good food."

"Can you guys stop talking about me as if I wasn't here?"

"If you answered the doctor's questions, we wouldn't have to," Callum snapped back.

She wanted to grab hold of those wide, strong shoulders and shake him. But she doubted she'd make any impact on him. It would take a disaster of biblical proportions to rattle him.

Doctor Cooper looked first at Gemma and then Callum. "Perhaps, Callum, you wouldn't mind giving us a quarter of an hour on our own while I go through a few things with Miss Winters."

It seemed that something other than brute force could move Callum—a doctor's raised eyebrow.

"Fifteen minutes." Callum looked from the doctor back to Gemma. "Fifteen minutes," he repeated like some kind of warning.


Callum walked out of the doctor's office and onto the road that led to the lake. What the hell was she playing at? Didn't she care about the baby? Why all the secrecy around her childhood? She'd told him her parents had died. What else was she trying to hide?

It was mid morning and the small town was busy with locals and tourists going about their business. He nodded in greeting to the people he knew but didn't stop to talk. He was rarely in the mood for talking, never more so than today.

He didn't stop walking until he reached the lake. There were few people on the lake at this hour of a weekday. Weekends in summer it could be busy with water sports, but now he could enjoy the emptiness of the blue expanse, framed by swathes of pink and purple lupins, the canopy of beech trees that barely moved under the hot summer sun, and the mountains. The light was sharp and bright, but filtered under the trees. He moved out from under the trees and squinted up at the bright white of the sun-capped Alps that fringed the skyline. He didn't shelter from anything. Faced it head on. Just like Gemma was going to have to do.

He didn't want to marry, not after what happened with

Claire. But he had no choice. He felt, at some deep, irrational level, it was a chance to replay history, to do what he should have done all those years ago, look after his wife and unborn child and make sure they lived. This time he'd do it right. Except this time it would be harder because he'd be marrying a secretive, diminutive, impractical redhead.

But he *would* acquire the land. That thought always sat at the front of his mind. It would mean he could regain the land his grandfather had lost in a card game, land that his great great grandfather had worked his butt off to buy. The Glencoe estate would be whole once more. He turned away from the peaceful lake scene. It was a solution to a long-term problem. Then why did it feel so wrong?

He glanced at his watch. The fifteen minutes was up. He swiftly retraced his steps, knocked at the door and waited impatiently for the doctor's response before entering his office. He looked from the doctor to Gemma and narrowed his gaze. Something had happened. Gemma appeared almost relaxed.

"You're in time for the scan." The doctor didn't look up but continued to fiddle with the monitor.

"Is it necessary?" Callum suddenly felt uncomfortable as Gemma lifted her top to reveal her stomach and the doctor began applying gel.

The doctor nodded. "Not always, but in this case, definitely."

Callum stood impatiently over them both.

"Sit down, Callum."

Callum ignored the doctor's instruction and remained standing. He'd leave. This was a waste of his time. Then the doctor wielded the scanner across Gemma's stomach, which shone with lubricant, and Callum swallowed. He looked away, focusing on the small monitor, anything so as not to see the expanse of bare skin. His hands itched to replace the doctor's scanner. He clenched them hard.

Then suddenly he saw something. He pointed to the screen, completely absorbed. "What the hell's that?"

"*That* is your baby, Callum."

"But, but—"

He swore under his breath as the unmistakable form of a baby suddenly came into view. "Is that a—"

"No, it's a leg." The doctor moved the scanner around a few more times. "We can't see the sex at the moment."

"Way to go on anatomy, Callum." Gemma's smile was full of humor and relaxed for once. She was as struck by the image before them as he was.

Callum suddenly felt weak. He sat down beside her, pointing to the screen, ignoring her sarcasm. "Is everything okay? It looks a strange shape."

"It's all fine. It's just the angle." The doctor shifted the scanner slightly. "There, now you can see a little better."

Callum didn't know where the huge lump came from but it formed in his throat and no amount of swallowing would remove it. He glanced down and found he was gripping Gemma's hand. He also saw that she was looking at him strangely, yet she'd made no effort to remove her hand from his and he didn't withdraw it.

He looked up at the doctor. "So, if you can't see the sex, what's so important about us viewing the scan?"

The doctor smiled and this time it reached his eyes. "It's not always about the physical, Callum." The doctor turned to Gemma. "There's a few things I'd like to discuss with Callum, if you wouldn't mind waiting outside, Gemma?"

Callum frowned as he watched Gemma leave the room. Experience told him his family's doctor was about to give him a lecture.

"Dr Cooper was better than I thought."

"He's been our family doctor for years. He knows his stuff. What were you talking about with him?"

"Just about my pregnancy. How I've been keeping and other stuff."

"Such as?"

"Just family stuff."

"I know about your parents, Gemma, you told me. What else haven't you told me?"

He felt the surprised glance, even though he kept his eyes straight ahead.

"There's little to tell."

"Then why don't you tell me? Where were you before you came here? What made you come here, what made you leave everything behind?"

He glanced at her and she appeared even paler if anything.

"You've got me living with you, you've got me marrying you, you're going to be a father to our child. Leave me something. My past is my own."

"It couldn't have been easy growing up with only a father. Where did your mother go to?"

She shrugged. "I don't know. I've never been told. All I know is that I don't want to be like her."

"I think you're more like her than you know." He could see the shock in her face.

"I'd never abandon my child. Never. I know what's it's like not to be loved. I won't inflict that on my child."

"I didn't say you would. But, there's a part of you—like it or not—that you've inherited from her. A thirst for adventure—a need to escape?"

"I'm *not* my mother."

"So you'll do the right thing, stay with me because of the child?"

"That's right."

Not because of any feelings she had for him. But he knew that already. She'd made that abundantly clear. All this stuff about needing to be free was just another way of telling him she had no feelings for him. Well, that was fine because he'd done with love. But she was to be the mother of his child—his wife—and he'd make good the doctor's suggestions of giving her her own space at Glencoe, even if he couldn't see the point in it.

Gemma was relieved Callum didn't feel the need to break the silence of their journey back to Glencoe. Seeing the baby on the monitor had stunned them both. But, she suspected, for different reasons.

For her, it made it so real. Despite all she said, she was scared of the child growing inside her. Scared she wouldn't be able to care for it, scared she wouldn't be able to do her best for it. Callum might think whatever he wanted, but it was fear that was driving her into this marriage.

She glanced at him, grim faced behind the sunglasses, his mouth a straight line. Whereas, Callum, she suspected, was simply relieved. The baby was well. Gemma had been sorted out. Another thing ticked off his list. All under control.

But why he'd gripped her hand when he saw the baby, she had no idea. Some instinctive need to connect with her? She dismissed the idea immediately. Callum didn't do "connect." He didn't seem to need any form of emotional engagement whatsoever.

She shifted her head on the headrest and looked at the unvarying golden plains. She suddenly saw her life rolling onwards forever, as blank as the plain that looked back at her. She closed her eyes.

She must have dozed off because she woke suddenly when the car pulled into the driveway. She opened her eyes to find Callum staring at her.

"We're home."

"Home..." she repeated, with a faint huff of laughter.

"You were tired."

"Umm. Long hours, difficulty sleeping."

"Doc said you'd been stressed. He suggested I do something about it."

"Like what?"

"Come with me. I've got something to show you."

They walked around the rear of the stables to a large barn. Callum pushed open the doors and stood aside for her to enter. It was a vast space with double height doors at each end, closed now, but presumably large enough for farm equipment to enter. The roof space was open with oak beams soaring up to the center beam like a medieval hall.

"It's beautiful."

"It's yours if you want it. I'll have it renovated. You can use it for your art studio."

Gemma froze. "Mine?" She didn't think he'd even have heard the word, she'd uttered it so quietly. She turned to look at him. "Mine?" she repeated.

He nodded. "Doctor Cooper said you needed your own space. I guess he's right. You can have this if you want it."

She swallowed, looking around the soaring space. She shook her head in disbelief.

Callum frowned. "I know it's dark at the moment. We

can have the double doors on both sides replaced with glass and windows punched in the side wall."

She couldn't turn to him but looked up at the ceiling, willing the tears to disappear. Surreptitiously she swiped them from her eyes and nodded her head. "That would be great." It seemed such a small thing to say in response to something as big as this.

"Hey, don't get upset. I'm sorry it's a bit rough. But it'll be okay."

She pressed her lips firmly together, willing herself not to break down. "It's perfect." Her voice was hoarse.

"It's just a studio."

She shook her head but didn't reply. She couldn't begin to tell him what it was he'd given her because he'd given her something far more than a mere studio. He'd given her something she'd never had before—consideration.

"And if you want to go out and about, I'll get Morgan to take you. It's a big country. I don't want you out on your own but I don't want you to feel trapped either. I want you safe, not trapped. Just make sure you always take Morgan with you. I trust him."

"Thank you."

"You're welcome. Just take care." He paused. "Of the baby."

She smiled. She was beginning to understand him now. "Dinner, tonight?"

She felt hopeful for the first time since she'd discovered she was pregnant. Perhaps there was something that could be gleaned from the wreckage of their relationship. He'd shown he was kind, thoughtful. They just needed time now. And they had plenty of that.

He lifted his hand to her face and cupped her cheek. "Sure."

. . .

Dinner with his wife to be. Callum watched her walk away, the spring in her step, the long red hair swinging around her back, her small, but rounded figure walking up to the house and he felt an ache for her that went too deep for comfort. He turned away and walked to the office. He couldn't go there again, particularly not with Gemma. Claire had wanted to be cared for and he had. Until that day when she'd insisted she spend the night in Christchurch alone. What no one else knew was that she'd been pregnant. He'd let her go, given her the space she said she'd wanted. The fire investigators had said it was faulty wiring that had caused the blaze that had killed her. But it wasn't. It was his own negligence—he should never have let her go. Particularly when it was discovered she hadn't been alone, not even in their apartment. He doubted the pain of loss and betrayal would ever leave him.

No. He'd do what he had to do for Gemma but he couldn't allow anyone to want more from him than he could give.

There'd be no dinner tonight. He had to get away.

———

It was early evening and Gemma sat on the swing chair on the side verandah that looked out across the wide expanse of the Glencoe estate. She'd had a long sleep in the afternoon and had awoken refreshed and with a new optimism. She'd dressed with care and was looking forward to dinner with Callum. She'd enjoyed the day, being with him, seeing her baby. She felt hopeful for the first time. Maybe, just maybe it would turn out okay.

Then she'd received the second postcard. Of course it was from Sarah. Who else would have sent it? But just the possibility that it was someone else, that it was Paul, sent a chill to her heart. No. It would have to be Sarah. She tapped the blank postcard she'd received that morning from Los Angeles. Still blank. Sarah clearly trusted no one with messages. What was she doing? Holidaying? It was strange that the intermittent postcards were coming closer to New Zealand. It surely didn't mean she was going to come here and claim her inheritance? It wasn't what she'd wanted, it wasn't in keeping with her character.

Gemma's musing were interrupted by the sound of a plane's engine. She frowned.

"Miss Winters?"

She turned to find Maria standing by the door.

"Mr. Mackenzie wished me to tell you that he's had to go to Wellington for a few days. He was looking for you this afternoon to tell you himself, but you were sleeping and he didn't like to disturb you."

Disappointment bit deep. She'd thought they'd made some ground today. It was the first time they'd spoken easily and she'd felt something of the old spark of warmth between them. She'd obviously been wrong.

"Thanks, Maria."

"You'll be requiring dinner in the dining room?"

She mustered up a weak smile. "No thanks. I'll eat it here."

"Certainly." Maria left.

She walked to the edge of the verandah and looked out. Across the green oasis of the garden, the cropped pastures gave way to an arid sun-dried airstrip, just big enough for Callum's plane. She watched it turn at the end of the valley and pick up speed for takeoff. The roar of the plane filled the valley.

Her husband-to-be was on that plane. And she hadn't a clue when he was returning or who he was going to be with.

She hardly knew him. She certainly didn't know the circles he moved in. Their own small part of the South Island was only a fraction of his world. There could very well be a woman, tucked away, awaiting his pleasure. Who was she? Was she important to Callum? Was she long term? And was he flying to be with her now?

She sighed. It wasn't meant to have been this way. She looked away as the plane soared off into the sky and she took in a gulp of the fresh air overlaid with a waft of engine fuel. Well, if he was maintaining his independence, so damn well was she. She had a life to get on with. She watched a group of men, including Morgan, walk back to the stables and garages.

And her life began here. Tomorrow.

# CHAPTER SEVEN

Callum tuned out from the conversation that centered on his young brother's, James's, latest amorous exploit, and looked around the dinner table at his family and friends. James, as usual, charmed and entertained everyone with his anecdotes. But James's stories were of no interest to him tonight, or only in as much as they delayed an inquisition into his own love life. Because Callum knew everyone was curious about recent events at Glencoe. No doubt his mother hadn't wasted any time in sharing the news.

Dallas, his elder brother, cast pointed glances at Callum from time to time. His old friends Guy and Lucia shot him the occasional amused look, while Cassandra, Dallas's wife, simply looked at him with sympathy. He didn't know which was the most alarming. Well, they'd all have to wait. He wasn't James, and he wouldn't be holding forth about his own love life, no matter what they wanted.

He sighed and gazed out, beyond Dallas, to the lights of Wellington that sparkled like jewels around the dark harbor. He tried to focus on the flashing light of an advertising hoarding, but the distant bronze-gold shimmer instead conjured up the image of a beautiful redhead, whose brown eyes became a kind of gold in certain lights—like the color of demerara sugar—a mouth-watering contrast to her creamy skin. He licked his lips as his mind drifted away, further still. Suddenly he felt a tugging at his ankles and looked down under the table to see Lily, Dallas's daughter, demanding his attention.

"So, what's all this about you getting married?" Dallas leaned back on the leather chair and slipped his arm around Cassandra.

Cassandra punched him lightly on the arm. "I told you to leave it to me."

Dallas glanced over at his wife with an amused smile. "You had an hour and you made no headway." He sipped his coffee. "I decided the direct approach would be more effective."

Callum extricated himself from Lily, who made a grab for the dog instead. Callum was no good with children, he didn't have a clue what to do with them and he didn't understand why Lily didn't get that. Instead, she always made a beeline for him.

Lucia smiled. "You may as well come clean. What's been going on?"

Irritated he glanced around the table. James, Lucia and Guy, Dallas and Cassandra were all grinning at him as if he'd done something vastly entertaining.

"What's been going on, Uncle Callum?" Lily parroted, grinning up at him with a gap-toothed smile from under the table. She was tying a pink ribbon around a border collie—a pup from Glencoe—who gazed up at Callum with mournful eyes. Callum shook his head in helpless sympathy and looked back up at Dallas.

"Gemma and I are to be married. We're expecting a baby in June. What more is there to say?"

"Well, nothing much except, how the hell did that happen?" Dallas could barely suppress his amazement. "I thought mother must have got it wrong. Since Claire, you'd sworn never to marry. Let alone have children."

"If it's the future of Glencoe you're worried about—"

"Of course not. James and I have got more than our hands full with other business interests. Glencoe has always been for you and your heirs." Dallas sat back. "At least you'll *have* some heirs now."

Cassandra leaned forward and laid her hand on Callum's. Callum could never resist his beautiful sister-in-law—so strong, so smart. He'd listen to her, above his brothers, any day. "Are you happy?"

The question cut through his defenses. He opened his mouth to speak but nothing came out. He cleared his throat, aware that everyone was looking at him. "It's what I want."

She smiled gently. "That's not what I asked."

"I...I can't remember happy. Not since Claire..."

Dallas stood up and walked over to get the bottle of wine and the decanter of whisky for Callum. Not that Dallas ever drank, but he refilled everyone else's glass. "It's about time you moved on. No point moping over something you have no control over."

"Dallas!" Both Lucia and Cassandra exclaimed at the same time.

"He's right," Callum said. "And I *am* moving on."

"So what's she like?" Lucia asked.

"Shorter than you. Slim." Callum shrugged.

Dallas, James and Guy shook their heads while the women exchanged amused glances. "You've just described half the population of women in the world," Guy said.

"Well, I don't know. She's just, *Gemma*. You'll see when you meet her."

"So the wedding really is next month? What's the rush?"

"There's no point in delaying. I want it sorted."

"Do you know if the baby's a boy or a girl?" Lucia bit her lip as if annoyed with herself for asking, for showing her interest. Callum relented a little. He knew Lucia and Guy had been trying for a baby for a long time and had had no luck so far. It couldn't be easy to watch Callum about to become a father.

"No. Gemma had a scan but it wasn't clear enough to see the sex." He hesitated, remembering how seeing the tiny image on the screen had moved him. "It was strange."

Guy and Dallas laughed. "Who'd have thought it? Callum Mackenzie getting emotional about a baby!"

"Okay!" Cassandra sighed, trying to shut them up, obviously aware of Lucia's feelings. "So tell us about Gemma. Where's she from?"

"England."

"Right. And her family? Are they coming over?"

"No, she doesn't have any."

"Oh." She opened her eyes wide in surprise. "That's sad. So she must be feeling very alone."

He shrugged in response.

"Don't you care?" Dallas asked.

"Look, cut out the inquisition, will you? Of course I care."

"No, Cassandra's right." Dallas leaned forward. "It *is* sad. What the hell are you doing here when she's all alone at Glencoe, in the middle of nowhere?"

"She's okay. She's pretty self-sufficient."

Dallas scoffed. "A case of having to be, I reckon."

"I've got business in Wellington."

"Nothing you couldn't have done from Glencoe."

"And there's the charity event at the museum tomorrow night."

"What?" Dallas shook his head in disbelief. "You never go to those things unless there's a woman you want there. And that can't be so in this case. Can it?"

Callum rubbed his hand over his face. "No of course not. I just thought I'd go for once."

"Sounds to me as if you wanted to escape for a while."

"I don't run away from things." A heavy silence followed in which he realized that that was just what he'd done. "Not usually..."

"Looks like you have now. And what about Gemma? All alone with only mother lurking nearby. You didn't tell mother to visit her, did you?"

"You know Gemma's met mother already."

"And she still wants to marry you?" The others laughed.

"Of course she does. She knows it's sensible."

"Jeez, mate. You really are the last of the romantics, aren't you?"

"You can talk!" Cassandra shot Dallas a glare. "Anyway, back to Gemma. Are you sure she's okay?"

"She's fine. She doesn't expect anything."

"Perhaps that's because she's never received anything." Cassandra paused. "Sounds to me as if you've done things the wrong way around. How about wooing her, how about giving her some of your time and company and seeing what comes of that?"

Cassandra was the only person he'd have accepted advice from. She'd been through a lot, he knew. And he'd admired the way she'd taken charge, had gone after what she'd believed in.

"Maybe."

Everyone laughed.

"I think, Cassandra my love," Dallas kissed his wife on the cheek, "coming from Callum, that's enthusiastic agreement!"

Callum sighed and pushed his glass forward. "Shut up and pour me a drink."

---

Callum landed the plane in a cloud of dust and taxied to the hangar. It was late afternoon and the sun still beat down. Out of habit he glanced at the state of the grass, noting it was already being leached of its moisture by the unrelenting summer sun. But he gave it no further thought as he focused on the house, focused on the one person in the house who had dominated his thoughts since he'd been away. He'd hoped that putting distance between them would give him some peace. But it hadn't.

She must have heard the plane land but there was no sign of her. He strode up to the house and looked around the downstairs then went up to the bedrooms. He hesitated by her bedroom, knocked and, receiving no reply, opened the door and breathed in deeply. He smelled her perfume. He smelled her. He missed her. As he came downstairs he was met by Maria.

"Have you seen Miss Winters?"

"Yes sir. She's gone out."

"And taken Morgan with her, I hope."

"Not that I know of, sir."

He scowled. *Typical.* "Where was she headed?"

"Well you know how interested in history she is—"

Callum grunted—a sound that could be taken either

way because he had no idea she was interested in history. His damn staff knew more about Gemma than he did. But then he'd made sure he'd kept his distance, hadn't he? He had to face the fact that he didn't know Gemma at all and that was down to him.

"I was telling her about how the Church of the Good Shepherd came into being," continued Maria, "and she wanted to have a look. Safe enough road, sir."

Callum strode across the drive, heading for his Range Rover. Maria was right, but only up to a point. The Mackenzie country weather was unpredictable and he'd told Gemma to always make sure Morgan was with her and she hadn't. It was for her own good. He could feel her slipping away from him already. Just as Claire had.

———————

Gemma lifted the old iron latch of the church with a clunk and pushed the groaning door inward. She stepped inside and inhaled the smell of polished wood and fresh flowers. It was cool and soothing—and she needed soothing. She'd thought that being close to Callum and unable to touch him, to hold him, as she'd wanted to was murder. But being away from him was worse.

She pushed the door closed and looked around. The church was old by New Zealand standards, about 1870. Built by Mackenzie country pioneers of lakeside boulders with an oak-shingled roof, it sat beautifully in its surroundings. The inside was just as impressive, simple, solid and light, with its cream plastered walls holding up the massive dark wooden beams.

She walked up the aisle, her eyes drawn above the stone altar to a window that gave views out over Shelter Lake and the mountains beyond. It was beautiful. Maria had told her that Gemma's ancestors and Callum's had been among the early settlers who had built the church. Of course, it hadn't been *her* ancestors. It had been Sarah's. But she couldn't say anything. Not if she wanted to keep up the façade and, if she didn't want to be found here by Paul, she had no choice.

Her hands traced the rugged carving of Christ on the front of the altar.

"My ancestor carved it. Yours designed it."

Shocked, she turned to see Callum standing quietly behind her. His large presence seemed to make the small church even smaller. She took a long slow breath to calm her pounding heart. "A marriage made in heaven then."

"Aren't they all?"

She raised an eyebrow. "Some have more pragmatic beginnings." She looked back at the carving. "But maybe they get there eventually."

She heard him exhale behind her, as if he'd been holding his breath. He walked up to her and took hold of her hand, pushing it towards the other relief carvings.

"Edelweiss, you see, and mountain lilies. And over here," he stretched her hand to the far side, "are keas. The settlers were fascinated by them."

"Keas?" Gemma frowned.

"Mountain parrots the size of a large owl, inquisitive and therefore easy prey for hungry settlers." He pulled her hand away but still held it tight as he slipped his hand around her waist. "You see the bronze candlesticks? They were sent from the men and women working The Grampians sheep station. They match the bronze cross. Bronze, oak, stone."

"As solid as the pioneers had to be."

He pulled her over to the oak stand. "You see here? The

stand and the Book of Remembrance have the Mackenzie country pioneers' names inscribed."

"I love that. It's as much about them as God." She laughed. "Your forebears must have been an arrogant lot. I can see where you get it from."

"*Your* forebears too, don't forget. You're pretty stubborn yourself, but perhaps not as arrogant."

Gemma swallowed. He was close to her now. So close she wouldn't have to move to kiss him. "Callum?"

"Mmmm?" he hadn't taken his eyes off her.

"How was Wellington?"

He pulled away as if he'd forgotten where he was. "Fine. Business. Family. What did you get up to?"

"Morgan's taken me out a couple of times, shown me around. They've started work on the studio and Morgan's brought my paintings over. Otherwise, I've just been hanging around Glencoe."

"Well," he said, turning back to her. "You look better for it."

"I feel better."

"Mother says the wedding arrangements are all made."

"Right. Christchurch, then?"

"Yep."

"Reception at some posh hotel?"

"You got it."

She took a deep breath. "I don't want that."

"It's family tradition."

"And does family tradition include marrying someone you don't love for the sake of their child?"

"Probably. But those stories aren't passed down through family history."

"Why don't we break with tradition? Look around you. Look at this place. Wouldn't it be fabulous for a wedding?"

"It's tiny. It wouldn't hold a quarter of the people mother wants to invite. She sent me the list last night."

"Let's make it just family and close friends. It's a farce. Why make it a public farce?"

"It's not a farce, Gemma. It's a practical solution to a problem."

She shook her head. "Then this church would also be practical. It's close to Glencoe. We could have the reception in the grounds there. Why not?"

He nodded. "I'd prefer it, too."

"Then let's do it."

"We'll have to fight that out with mother. But, for what it's worth, I agree.'

The tension in Gemma was released and she smiled and leaned against his shoulder. "Thank you. I don't want a big wedding in Christchurch to suit other people—people your mother wants to impress. Only—"

"Yes?"

"To..." She wanted to tell him that she wanted the wedding to mean something to them, *just* them. But she wasn't sure it *did* mean anything to Callum.

"To suit *our* needs."

"I guess, yes. Whatever they are. And I have a funny feeling they're different for both of us."

"Maybe. Maybe not." She felt her hopes rise at the way he held her hand. It wasn't like Paul had, gripping her wrist like a shackle, hurting her. No, for all his controlling ways, Callum had never once made her feel trapped. He held her hand gently within his own large, strong hand, as if he were cradling a bird. "Come on. Let's go."

He pulled her outside into the fresh air. The afternoon wind had risen, whipping the hot dry air around them. The orange-red fruits of the coprosma and buttercup daisies were bright with the fiery sun. Two large paradise ducks squawked their annoyance at the intrusion and flapped a little further away onto the lake. Wekas, pukeko and bittern lifted their long skinny legs delicately around the swamp area surrounding the lake as gray ducks and gulls soared in the bright blue sky, buoyed by the rising wind. Surrounded by such beauty, her hand held by the man she felt so much for, despite the fact his stubborn, arrogant nature insisted he remain a stranger, she felt a flare of hope ignite and refuse to subside.

She stopped by a gravestone. "Look at these names. Perhaps we should look for inspiration." She peered at one. "Violet Rose. How about that?"

"I think something more ordinary." He nodded to another gravestone. "Like Joan, or Mary."

She laughed and pulled him away. "Okay. Discussion looming, but not now."

He groaned and pulled her tightly towards him. "I've missed you, Gemma."

"It was you who went away."

"Yes, well. I did have work..."

"But you didn't *have* to go away, did you?"

"No. I was finding it difficult, being with you, but not being with you, if you know what I mean."

"And now? Still difficult?"

He smiled a slow, secretive smile that melted her body, from the inside out. She drew in a long, slow breath and held it, wanting to know what lay behind that smile. He shook his head and she let out the breath. "No."

She touched a golden curl that shone in the sun and tried to tuck it, in vain, behind his ear. She slid her palm against his cheek, feeling an overwhelming tenderness and sadness at the same time. "Callum, I've missed you too.

That first time we were together, it was everything I'd always wanted. I couldn't believe I was so happy. And then, it vanished and I knew it had been too much to expect." She twisted her hand round, and stroked the back of her fingers against his stubbly chin. "Tell me, is it dangerous for me to expect something now?"

"We're marrying. You're expecting our child. No doubt I could have done the whole thing better, but we *are* going to be together. Expect that."

How could she change the habit of a lifetime and expect something good? She shook her head. "You've not answered my question." She searched his face and saw the uncharacteristic uncertainty there. "I *know* our life will be together, I'm asking what kind of life it will be."

He touched her chin with his finger and lifted her face to his. "It *will* be okay. I promise you." He brushed her lips with his thumb as if he wanted to kiss them but was unsure of her reaction.

She folded her hands around his and pressed them against her mouth. He slipped his fingers into her hair and kissed her. His lips barely moved over hers but coming out of the blue, the kiss had a raw sensuality that was shocking. For one long moment they stayed there, both minds focused on nothing else but the sensation of their connection. Then, slowly, his mouth relaxed against hers and he pulled away. He kept his hands thrust in her hair, framing her face, and held his face close. "It will be *more* than all right. I care for you, Gemma."

She nodded. Coming from anyone else it would have been a bland, ambiguous statement. Coming from Callum, it was practically a declaration of love. Practically, but not quite.

He slipped his arm around her shoulders. "Come on.

Let's get back. It's getting late." He grinned. "We'll have to work out how to break the news to mother of our change of wedding venue. Or *who* will break the news."

She laughed and whispered in his ear. "Last one home gets to tell your mother."

———

Paul McCarthy sat in the private alcove of his London nightclub, surrounded by the small group of people he kept close by his side at all times. With his business interests it didn't pay to ever be alone, to ever be vulnerable. He'd inherited his patch of London from his father who'd lost his life in an uncharacteristic moment of softness. Paul had learned from that. His men had to have two attributes: blind loyalty and no morals. Simple.

The blonde with a generous bottom and even more generous bust wriggled on his lap, demanding attention. He could have her here and now, despite the people all around him. She wouldn't care. Women like her didn't. That, unfortunately, was the downside of surrounding oneself with people with no moral compass. *That* was why he so cherished Gemma. She'd been different, she'd been his Princess. Something or someone had taken her away. He knew where she was. It hadn't taken long to find her. He knew she was living by herself and he'd given her time to realize her mistake. He'd considered taking the first plane to her and bringing her home but he knew she'd realize what a big mistake she'd made sooner or later. Paul McCarthy didn't run after women. Women ran to him. And Gemma would too. He'd sent her little reminders of him, just so she knew.

Paul glanced up as one of his men sat down beside him. The man pushed an envelope across the table to Paul.

Paul scanned the contents, then reread it, disbelieving. He neatly refolded the report and placed it back in the envelope. The music in the club receded to a dull repetitive thud, pounding in time to the roar of blood pulsing heavily through his veins.

*Married? What the hell?* There'd been no sign of any other man. The woman wriggled once more on his lap while his man looked at her appreciatively. Fury licked through his veins. He could hardly think straight. Gemma was the only woman he wanted. Yes, he could have any woman but there was only one woman whom he loved, who he didn't want to share.

"You want her?" he said pushing the blonde off his lap. "Have her." The blonde fell laughing on top of the man whose hands swept up under her dress, revealing the tops of her thighs and more. But the man's eyes were still on Paul. Business first.

"You want me to go and bring Gemma back to you?"

"No." Paul's intense gaze was fixed with disgust on the woman's bare flesh—she wore no underwear. She was nothing but a slut. Some women were like that. But not Gemma. She'd been a virgin when he'd met her and they'd had something special. He'd even begun to think about marriage before she disappeared. Disappeared without trace. Or so she'd thought.

And now, some man had got his hands on his Gemma? A blood red mist passed over his eyes. The report said she was pregnant. But he didn't believe that. She wouldn't let anyone touch her. Only him. That was the way it had been. "No," he repeated. "I'll go. Send her another blank post-card. This time from Auckland. It'll let her know I'm coming, that I'm closer. She'll be ready then."

# CHAPTER EIGHT

"So, Lady Mackenzie, we won't be getting married in Christchurch after all."

Gemma's confident reflection in the dining room mirror stared back at her. Callum stood behind her, a smile twitching on his lips.

"That won't cut it, Gemma. You'll have to try harder than that."

"Okay, how about this." She bobbed down on one knee. "My lady." She looked up with an impish grin. "Callum has something he'd like to say to you." But her grin faded when she saw the look in his eyes. He wasn't listening to her. His mouth had softened and his eyes strayed around her face and hair before settling on her lips.

"That's right, pass the buck." He extended his hand to hers. Slowly she rose to her feet and he pulled her to him. "But it's you who wants to marry here, at Glencoe. Why should I risk my mother's wrath?"

"You may find it in your interests to help a girl out here."

"Is that right?"

"Umm."

A spark of humor warmed his blue eyes. "And what particular interests would they be?"

She broke his gaze and smoothed down his dinner jacket. "Well, you'll have to find out, won't you? After you've been to Christchurch to see your mother."

"Are you sure you don't want to come?"

"Honestly? I think this conversation is best between the two of you. I'll be here. When you return tomorrow."

He stepped towards her. "What are you going to do?"

"I'm," she paused for dramatic flourish, "going to go to bed."

He brushed his hand under her eyes. "You don't look tired."

"I'm not."

He groaned again. "I'll give mother a call and postpone it. If I have dinner with her this evening, I won't be able to return here tonight."

She pushed him away. "No, you go. Get it over with. I'll see you tomorrow."

———

Gemma awoke with a start, her heart racing as she gasped for breath. She sat bolt upright, her eyes wide as she looked around, trying to work out what had woken her up. The only movement was the flick of the open curtains in the breeze through the sash window. Moonlight flooded the room, bathing her naked body in its white light. She swallowed and wiped her palms over her face trying to eradicate the image of the man who haunted her nights.

She'd been dreaming of Paul, that he'd called out to her that he was coming for her. He'd been staring at her, his eyes cold and fierce, furious and possessive. She shuddered in terror and repulsion. She pulled herself up out of the disheveled sheets and leaned against the pillow. A slick of cool sweat covered her face and shoulders where the chill breeze touched her. Would the nightmares never leave her?

But what had awoken her? Her ears pricked at some small sound, her senses alert and straining. There it was again: the clunk of a foot meeting the brass rod that held back the old-fashioned carpeting on the stairs. Then the footfall became lost again in the runner of carpet that stretched along the length of the landing. But she could swear she could still hear it, coming towards her—a soft muffled heaviness that stopped right outside her door.

Callum was staying overnight in Christchurch. It was too dangerous to fly into Glencoe at night and too far by road. It was Paul. It had to be. He'd tracked her down. The door slowly opened and she saw a dark shape enter the room and close the door quietly, with a soft click. She couldn't see who it was and he made no sound. But she was plainly visible, sitting in the pool of moonlight.

She pulled the sheets up around her and wriggled away from the intruder. The man stepped towards her. "Keep away from me or I'll scream!"

A hand reached out to her but all she could do was open her mouth in a silent scream, frozen in the moonlight.

"Gemma! It's only me. Callum." She collapsed against him, shaking, unable to speak a word. He pulled her to him and wrapped her in his arms. She breathed in his familiar male smell—it *was* him, it was Callum. Not Paul. "What's the matter? Bad dream?"

She nodded her head against his chest as she tried to rid her mind of the image of the man who haunted her, who she doubted now, would ever leave her nightmares. "Real bad."

"Anything you want to talk about?"

Slowly her heart thudded back to normal. Surreptitiously she wiped her tears with the back of her hand and took a deep breath. She pulled back. "No. It's nothing."

"Didn't sound like nothing." He held her at arm's length as he tried to decipher the truth from her expression. But she couldn't tell him. To begin with she'd been too scared to tell anyone her secret in case Paul got to hear of her whereabouts. Now she trusted Callum and she knew her secret would be safe with him. But Callum was marrying her, believing her to be Gemma Winters, heiress of Blackrock, descendant of Mackenzie country pioneers, like he was. Callum didn't strike her as the sort of person who would easily accept deceit. There wasn't a dishonest bone in his body. He'd rather devastate with the truth than save his soul by lying. She, on the other hand, couldn't devastate with the truth. Her baby's future depended on it.

"Just a bad dream," she repeated. She sucked in a difficult breath. "Anyway, what are you doing here? You said you'd be staying overnight in Christchurch."

"I decided to drive back. The thought of what was waiting for me here made a three-hour ride over rough roads bearable."

She grinned. "Is that so? And what exactly *is* waiting for you here? Is it a chat you're wanting?"

"Of course. That's exactly what I was thinking about every minute of that long ride home."

"Well, let's start with your mother, then. How did she take the news about the wedding?"

He shrugged. "She's fine."

She smiled then. "I bet she wasn't. You just don't want to talk about it."

He pushed a strand of hair back off her face. "You're getting to know me."

"Yes, I am. You're not hard to know, Callum."

He narrowed his eyes. "Am I so simple then?"

She cocked her head to one side and grinned. "Yes, actually. Simple, predictable."

He made a deep growling sound at the back of his throat. It was fun teasing him.

"Is that right?"

"Umm," she relented as he moved his mouth closer to hers and her eyes slipped to those lips, so sensuously carved in his otherwise strong face. "Yes, it is. That's what comes of being so damned solid and upstanding."

"Strange, a few weeks ago you called me controlling and arrogant."

"Yep, you're all that too. But that's like the top layer of your character, the annoying bit that everyone sees and some people—possibly myself included—judge you on. But under that layer is the bedrock that makes you so predictable. It's that bedrock that makes the controlling and arrogant bit less scary because I know it comes from something far more honorable."

"Honorable, I like."

"Me too."

Slowly he pushed his fingers into her hair and cupped the back of her head, bringing her lips even closer to his. "And the unpredictable?"

"Well, I'm sure with a little persuasion, we can work on that."

"And how do you propose to do that?"

She leaned towards him and touched his lips with hers. She pulled away and looked up into his eyes, hard and colorless in the white moonlight. She shifted further away, reminded once more of her nightmares.

He raised an eyebrow. "Is that it?"

The rumble of his voice in his chest, pressed against hers, cleared away the last traces of her nightmare. "Just warming up. There's more where that came from."

She lifted her fingers to his lips and touched them briefly to reassure herself further. They weren't Paul's hard, lean lips, pulled tight in barely controlled anger; Callum's were full of passion and generosity at that moment. In the cold light of day they appeared less generous but that was because she knew now that he was always under control. Or nearly always.

She replaced her fingers with her lips. She leaned into him once more, tasting him as her fingers had touched him. Still he made no move. She was determined to shatter his control. She flicked her tongue against his lips and they parted, allowing her entry. She reached her hand up to his chest where she felt the solid thump of his quickened heart-beat. He opened his mouth further and she smiled and pulled away. Who had control now?

"Umm, getting better. What next?"

Slowly she unbuttoned his shirt, concentrating on taking her time, on teasing him with her slowness and the occasional soft scratch of her nail against his chest, against his stomach and lower. Her hand rested on his belt. She continued to flick her tongue across and between his lips as she slid her hands around him. A shudder of deep longing ran through her body. She undid his belt and button and he pulled off his clothes.

He caressed her neck and collarbone, moving out to her shoulders, pushing the covers down until her naked body was revealed. He dipped his head and kissed the top of each breast before his mouth enveloped her exquisitely sensitive nipple. She gasped and plunged her fingers into his hair, the gold dimmed in the cool moonlight.

"I've missed you, Gemma." His hot breath heated her breasts as his hands moved down over her stomach, touching it reverently, gently caressing its roundness. "The baby, it's so hard to believe."

She smiled and leaned her cheek against his head. "Not for me. Either I'm pregnant or I have to go on a massive diet."

He lifted his head, his hands still around her stomach, and pressed his lips either side of her mouth. Her breath caught at his gentleness. He was so big and commanding that this tenderness was unexpected and excited her more than any show of raw machismo could.

She thrust her hands in his hair and held him close, their kiss deepening, their tongues tangling with an eroticism that made her rise until she was kneeling, naked, before him. His hands smoothed over her breasts, so much larger now that she was pregnant. She closed her eyes as he lay her down onto the white sheets beneath him.

It seemed he became more controlled as her excitement and need grew. He was careful not to lean his weight upon her, and his hands were gentle as they explored her body with a lightness of touch which created vivid curls of sensations deep inside. And that thoughtful consideration continued to devastating effect as he made love to her. With each passing second the coiling tensions inside grew tighter, the rhythm quickening until her body demanded release. And she got it.

In the intensity of that moment neither moved as they sought each other's eyes. In that instant Gemma could have sworn she felt what Callum was feeling. Then the moment passed, the contact was broken.

He rolled off her carefully, his hand trailing over her full, tight breasts, her stomach and her legs, before resting back on her stomach again. They lay for some minutes both looking up at the ghostly white ceiling, its plaster moldings highlighted by the moon shadows, listening to each other's breathing settle.

"You okay?"

"Of course. More than okay." She turned to look at Callum, thoughts tumbling through her mind. Should she tell him she was glad? Glad that he'd made love to her, glad that they'd breached the barrier that he'd erected since she'd arrived. It was all she wanted—him to love her and the baby. But before any words could form, he shifted his arm and pulled away.

Stunned, she lay back without saying anything, just watching the moonlight play on the wallpaper, the furnishings, just listening to his breathing. Long minutes passed and still neither said anything. He wasn't asleep. She knew he wasn't but she couldn't break the silence his physical separation had brought between them.

Then he swung his legs around and put his feet on the floor, his hands spiking up through his hair. He held his head briefly before standing up. He still didn't look at her.

"Where are you going?" Her words were a bare whisper.

"I'll be back." He sighed and plucked a robe off the back of the door. "I won't be long."

She didn't reply, just watched him go. The gap had been bridged, sure, but only briefly, only enough to make her realize that an even larger gap existed between them that had nothing to do with the physical. And she didn't have the first idea how to bridge that one.

Callum stood on the verandah looking across the dark land, listening to the soft wind playing in the trees behind the house and the occasional haunting territorial call of a more-pork owl. He'd wanted Gemma so much but he'd got more than he'd bargained for tonight. And he didn't have a clue how to handle the confusion of feelings that being close to her stirred within him. They made him vulnerable and he didn't do vulnerable.

He'd been so young when he'd married Claire and had loved and trusted her implicitly; he'd have given her anything she wanted. Turned out what she'd wanted was the thrill of the chase, not the actual commitment. Despite his doubts over her fidelity he'd let her go to Christchurch when she'd said she'd wanted to spend a few days in their apartment alone. He'd thought if he let her go, she'd get whatever was eating her out of her system and return to him. It wasn't until the police had contacted him that he'd discovered she hadn't been at their apartment, but at an old house that had had faulty electrical wiring. Claire had died in the fire, her lover had died and so had her unborn baby. He'd never know if it had been his baby.

The pain of love betrayed, of sheer empty loss—because he'd allowed it—still ached deep in his bones, a physical pain that he knew now would never leave. All he could do to put it right was protect himself by keeping separate from Gemma and protect her with the care and control he'd stopped himself from giving to Claire.

He walked slowly into the house and up the stairs, back into Gemma's bedroom and slipped under the covers beside her. There was no movement from her and he assumed she was asleep. He shifted to his side to face away from her. He couldn't turn back the clock. He had to face this new intimacy with Gemma but he also had to find a way of keeping himself separate—his emotions under control, safe.

---

It had been a week since they'd first made love at Glencoe—a week of intimate nights and days when they'd hardly seen each other—Callum had made sure of that. But the lonely days were beginning to take their toll.

He leaned back in his office chair and looked out across the land, trying to focus on the things that had always been constant in his life. Trying to focus on anything but Gemma. The sun had yet to rise and the trees and grass were clothed in a soft opaque mist. But he could see through the softness, noticing the dryness of the grass, the curled leaves on the trees—autumn had come early and was drier than normal. He'd have to tell his men to be more alert than usual to the ever-present danger of fire.

But even that threat was soon subsumed by thoughts of Gemma. He gritted his teeth and returned his focus to the computer. He wouldn't think of Gemma now, it was too unsettling. He felt it tugging at him, confusing him with his feelings. He didn't *do* feelings he reminded himself. Suddenly he felt a prickle of awareness rise up his back. He turned around. Gemma stood there, showered, dressed and with a determined look on her face. He groaned inwardly.

"Coffee?" He indicated the coffee on the table.

She shook her head. "No thanks. I've come here to talk."

The stone-like heaviness sunk further inside. "About anything in particular?"

"Yes, as it happens. About us."

"Really." He kept his voice cool, neutral.

"Is this how it's going to be? Nothing during the day, no civil talk, no intimacy, only passionate love-making at night?"

"Yes. What more do you want?"

"Talking might be nice. Sharing the odd meal would be"—she shrugged exaggeratedly—"I don't know, civil maybe?"

"I'm busy during the day. You know that."

"What I know is you're hiding behind your work."

"Don't be ridiculous. You wanted freedom in our marriage, you're getting it."

"That all changed when we became intimate at night. You know it did. How can we make love at night like we do and then act like complete strangers during the day, assuming I manage to catch a glimpse of you?"

"We just do it, that's how. Look, I've no time for this." His phone indicated the arrival of a text and he picked it up, thankful for the diversion. "It's from Cassandra. She says she and Lucia are setting up a hen's night for you next week. You don't want that, do you?"

"Yes, I do. I know about it. She rang me."

He frowned. "I hadn't taken you for a party animal."

"Just shows how little you know about me."

He remembered Claire's need to party, to be publicly—and privately it turned out—admired. "It's up to you."

"Yes, it is. That would be *my* freedom, wouldn't it? Freedom to do as I like, when I like, except at night, except when I'm in your bed, lying there, waiting for you. So long as I'm willing to have sex with you, you're happy aren't you?"

He narrowed his gaze. "That's crass, Gemma."

"Yes, it is, and it's the truth."

She was too close now. She lifted her hand to his face and smoothed her fingers around his temples, until her palm cradled his chin, her thumb brushing against his lips. He closed his eyes. She was too close, he felt too vulnerable. "Tell me, what are you feeling now? Do you still care for me, like you said you did?"

It took all his strength to open his eyes and take hold of her hand and drag it down to her side. "Yes, of course. But that's all. I've nothing more to give. Anything else died with Claire."

He saw the hurt slam into her, heat flushed her face, brightening her misting eyes and her lips trembled for one brief moment before she tightened her mouth into a hard line. He saw she was angry and braced himself for an onslaught that didn't come.

"You loved once. You can love again." Her voice was far softer than he expected. It was as if all the shouting remained inside, grinding into the hurt he could see, deepening it until it was raw and bleeding.

"No, it's not possible. I'm not made that way."

"Perhaps you're just marrying the wrong girl."

"I'm marrying the girl I need to marry. End of story." He didn't watch her leave, just heard the door close quietly behind her.

He'd done what he'd had to do, but at what cost?

The Lakehouse Café was humming. Music from the live band pounded through her body, escaping through the open windows out into the dark of the night. While Gemma wasn't exactly in the mood for dancing, she *had* been in the mood for getting out of Glencoe, which was now teeming with Callum's family and close friends. She'd dressed with care hoping that Callum would see her in the provocative dress that showcased her newly plump breasts but hid her swollen stomach. But he'd been conspicuous by his absence.

"Don't look so gloomy, let's dance." Lucia indicated the dance floor. Gemma grinned. Whatever her issues with Callum, she couldn't have asked for a lovelier sister-in-law than Cassandra or better friends than Lucia and Rebecca. Gemma jumped up and followed Lucia and Cassandra to the dance floor, grabbing Rebecca's protesting hand on the way.

"But, I don't dance," Rebecca shouted above the music.

"You do now." Gemma grinned.

Gemma stopped long enough for Rebecca to swig back her drink to give her courage. Gemma's grin widened as Rebecca pushed her glasses on her nose and self-consciously shifted from one leg to the other more or less in time to the driving beat. Rebecca was an academic through and through, it was about time she let that glorious hair down.

As soon as the music stopped, Rebecca made a beeline back to the table where she downed the glass of wine the waiter had refilled.

"Easy, Rebecca. You're not used to drinking."

Rebecca smiled unsteadily and unfocused. "No, but it's quite nice. Makes all of this"—she gestured around the club—"more manageable somehow."

Gemma laughed. "You should get out more often."

"I'm too busy. I need to have my new project proposal finished by next month if I'm to attract research grants."

Gemma let her mind drift. Research, schmesearch. It was all the same to her. Rebecca was a beautiful girl who had steadfastly resisted Gemma's attempts at matchmaking since she'd been in New Zealand. But now a new thought flitted through her mind. She palmed her forehead. Why hadn't she thought of it before? She got out her cell and rang Morgan.


"May I have this dance?"

Gemma turned to find Callum standing behind her—his tall, broad presence, unmoving amongst the swaying bodies.

"I'm not sure that's proper on a hen night."

"I don't think there's much 'proper' about us any more."

She couldn't contain a grin as he pulled her to him. "I guess you're right. So, tell me, why are you here?"

They swayed to the slow music for a while. "I wanted to make sure you were all right."

She groaned against his chest. "Didn't think you cared."

"I care about my own. And that's just what you are—what you will be."

She smiled shakily. "Care for me like you would one of your possessions."

"I didn't say that."

"But that's what you mean, right?"

"What does it matter? All you need to know is that I won't let anything happen to you."

"As extensive as you no doubt think your power is, I really don't think you're able to control everything." Least of all her own heart. He was breaking it with every word.

"Of course. I'm not God." He hesitated as his eyes searched her own for the truth. His thumb caressed her cheek. She tried desperately to hide her thoughts and her feelings but nothing could stop the electric response of her body to his touch. Her lips parted as his thumb dragged lazily towards them. "But I'll give him a run for his money."

She laughed aloud and Callum's mouth twitched in amusement.

He tilted her chin so she faced him. "That's more like it."

The laughter had banished the tension and their eyes locked. He narrowed his eyes in challenge as he moved closer to her. Her skin goose-bumped as his hands slowly stroked down her arms before shifting and coming to rest on the top of her hips. His hands hitched up her dress slightly until his fingers spread around her hips, his thumbs sliding down to rest in the groove between her swollen stomach and her hip bones, following the line of her underwear. A throbbing heat settled deep inside. His breath quickened against her cheek and the skin over the pulse in his neck betrayed his heart was beating as fast as her own.

He pulled her closer to him but suddenly his body tensed and he stepped away. "What's Morgan doing here?"

She followed his gaze. "Oh," she shrugged. "I called him."

"And why did you do that?"

Anger was evident in every syllable. She stood back and crossed her arms. She was about to reply in kind when Cassandra suddenly appeared.

"Callum, what on earth are you doing here? This is a hen's night, may I remind you." She shooed him away. "Off you go. You'll see Gemma soon enough tomorrow."

Callum watched as Cassandra grabbed one of Gemma's arms and Lucia another and playfully marched her away. He glanced once more at Morgan, who was sitting beside

Rebecca, neither of them talking, as they watched Gemma. What the hell was going on? Anger filled him. He'd been a fool to suggest Morgan accompany Gemma around the estate. Not because he didn't trust Morgan. It was Gemma he didn't trust. He'd been a fool to think Gemma was different from Claire. Claire had needed the flattery and attention of other men and so, it seemed, did Gemma. There was one thing he hadn't been a fool about and that was to keep her at an emotional distance.

He walked outside and breathed deeply of the night air.

---

Gemma sat, fully clothed on the chaise by the open window in her bedroom, listening to the morepork hooting his sweetly soft call over the valley, waiting for Callum to come. She'd have it out with him. They were to be married tomorrow. This couldn't go on. One face in public, the other in private. Physical intimacy with no emotional intimacy—she couldn't do it.

She glanced at her watch. It was late. Everywhere was quiet. She ran a glass of water and sipped it while she waited. At last she heard the sounds she was waiting for. Callum's footsteps. Theirs were the only bedrooms in that wing. It could only be him.

She frowned as the footsteps walked past her door. Surely he wasn't going to keep with tradition and not see her the night before the wedding? No. It wasn't that. He'd admitted he didn't care for traditions.

He'd come. He always came. But his footsteps kept on walking. The door closed and a heavy silence fell.

The sound of a single dog howling from a distant property across the valley underscored Gemma's sadness.

She rose wearily and faced herself in the bathroom mirror while she tipped the water down the sink. She looked at her reflection blankly as she took off her make-up before it could run. She didn't manage it. But it would be the last time. No more tears after tonight. Tomorrow, on her wedding day, she'd make him see.

# CHAPTER NINE

"...From this day forward until death do us part..."

The words sounded like a death knell to Gemma's ears, a life sentence. A deep fear, almost physical, rose up and tightened around her chest. She pushed away a strand of hair that clung cloyingly to her damp cheek, desperately trying to keep the panic at bay. She focused on Callum's jaw—the stubble, for once, absent—so everyone would think she was looking at him, everyone but Callum.

One quick glance revealed he was as cool as ever, unconcerned, and ruggedly handsome. The perfect man. Unfortunately it didn't seem she was the perfect woman for him.

Her life had turned into a mess of deceit and hypocrisy, just like her parents', just like Paul's—everyone fooling themselves they were doing the right thing, everyone hurting everyone else in the process. And Callum? For all his integrity, he was fooling himself most of all.

Gemma sucked in a long, slow breath, calming her fears and drawing the cooling strength of the fragrant air deep inside—a strength that transformed the fear into anger, the desperation into determination.

Gemma's eyelashes on her downturned gaze barely flickered in response to the Pastor's words. Callum saw her mind was elsewhere but it was only in her trembling hands, that he held in his, that he could sense the tension. Tenderness flooded his heart and he yearned to pull her to him in a hard, passionate kiss, to connect with her, just as he did by night when there was no distance between them. But he froze. He couldn't give her anything further. Seeing her at the café, watching her with Morgan, had aroused all the bitter feelings of jealousy and anger that he'd thought he'd buried with Claire. It had confirmed his need to retain control because he never wanted to feel that pain again.

"You may kiss the bride."

Callum reached over and lifted the veil from Gemma's face, revealing the delicate lines of her face under the soft light that filtered through the church windows. Her eyes lifted up to his, their soft brown now expressing a determination and challenge that hadn't been there before.

His mother coughed indiscreetly and he realized everyone was waiting for him to kiss the bride. He dipped his head and kissed Gemma chastely on the lips. He quickly pulled away, but couldn't take his eyes away from hers, where the determination was briefly replaced by hurt. But only briefly. She looked away and flashed a smile at everyone, embarrassed by his obvious coldness. The whoops and cheers and laughter filtered through to him, subdued as if they came from far away, as they both turned and walked down the aisle.

The Church of the Good Shepherd had been the

perfect choice. He'd caught Gemma looking at the altar and he knew she'd been remembering their afternoon together. They'd made a connection in the church. Something had sprung into life, fresh and young, but too tender. He'd squashed it before it could flower. If she was remembering that day, her expression was the opposite of the one he recalled. Her jaw jutted in determination, even as she smiled politely to everyone around her—a smile that wouldn't fool anyone who knew her, because her eyes were bright with the warning flare of anger.

Outside the church, the brilliant autumn light sparkled as clouds of confetti rained down on them both. Friends and family, together with curious locals, thronged around them.

"A kiss! A kiss!" the crowd shouted.

Callum turned to Gemma, his hand automatically reaching up to dislodge a piece of confetti caught in the sweep of red hair that was held in a loose knot at the nape of her neck. "A kiss, Mrs. Mackenzie?"

She leaned into him. "An inside kiss or an outside kiss?" Her whisper could only be heard by him.

He frowned. He knew she was referring to the difference between how they were in the bedroom to how they were in front of the rest of the world.

"As you like."

"Umm." That same flare deepened in her eyes, masking the anger with the unmistakable hunger of desire. She pulled his head towards hers and pressed her lips against his. She held him firm as she deepened the kiss, pushing her tongue against his. It was as if he'd been punched in the gut, depriving him of all his control—and he slid his tongue over hers, pressing his lips harder to hers, sinking his fingers into the soft curves of her body.

Then she pulled away, her eyes narrowed in triumph.

He stepped back and blinked as he realized where he was. But their eyes held. She'd issued a challenge. He shook his head slightly. It was a challenge she wasn't going to win. There was too much at stake.


"You've a beautiful bride, brother."

"As do you."

Callum and Dallas looked over to where their wives stood under the shade of a rose-covered pergola, one tall and dark, the other petite and red-headed. Their attention was completely absorbed by Lily's baby sister who laughed as Gemma produced a rattle from a different position behind her body each time. They could hear the baby's infectious chuckle from where they stood, echoed by the women's laughter.

"We're lucky men, Callum. Who'd have thought it a few years ago?"

"Certainly not me."

"Is everything okay with you and Gemma? Seems to me you've kept your distance. Haven't seen you touch her once, apart from that pathetic excuse for a kiss you gave her after the vows had been exchanged. Looks as though your new wife knows how to kiss though. What's all that about?"

"It's complicated."

"Complicated? Come on! I haven't been able to keep my hands off Cassandra since I met her—except for a few months when we were apart, which damn nearly killed me. But you seem too cool with Gemma."

"Cut the analysis. I'm not interested. It's an arrangement we're both happy with, so just leave it at that."

"An 'arrangement?' You cold-hearted bastard! Are you

telling me that it was only about the land? Some kind of deal? She gives you the land and she gets you?"

"Something like that."

"Bad deal on her part." Dallas pressed his lips together in a tight line as he struggled to keep quiet. He shook his head and sighed. "Look, Callum, life doesn't run smooth. *Love* doesn't run smooth—no-one knows that better than me. But there have been stranger beginnings to marriages that have ended up strong. All I'm saying is, give your marriage a chance. Don't kill it stone dead with indifference before it's begun."

Callum glared at his brother. "Quit lecturing me. I'm not interested."

"Not interested in what? Your marriage?" He shook his head, incredulous. "You've only just *got* married!"

"Look, Dallas. While you were out hellraising, I spent my teens being an emotional prop to our mother. I escaped into a marriage to a woman I loved which was cut short too soon. The last thing I need is some emotionally needy woman dragging me down."

He felt a light touch on his arm from behind and turned abruptly to see Gemma, her dress and veil billowing cloud-like in the breeze, emphasizing her slightness. Dallas groaned and stepped away.

"'Emotionally needy,' Callum?" Gemma's voice drifted across to him in a precise whisper. "And if I am, who made me that way? Who insisted on marriage, insisted on me giving up my job? Insisted on being there for *you*, just in case you decided you wanted me." Her eyes glittered. "The answer is *you*. And if you don't like what you've got, then I suggest you'd better make some changes." She narrowed her eyes that were almost black in the harsh overhead light and walked towards the house.

The sound of slow clapping made him turn around. Dallas had witnessed everything.

"Good one, Callum. You really know how to make your marriage work, don't you?"

"Shut it, Dallas."

Dallas fisted his hands and gritted his teeth. "Don't talk to me like that, mate. I don't want to end up throwing a punch at my brother on his wedding day."

Callum, distracted, as he watched Gemma disappear indoors, turned and saw his short-tempered brother's flash of anger. "Just like the old days, huh?" He shook his head. "Those days are over. If there's one thing we've both learned, it's control." He sighed.

"Darling! Over here please!" Lady Mackenzie was beckoning to one of them. They both looked around for James.

"Where the hell's the favorite son when you need him?" Dallas exclaimed. He'd swiftly recovered from the flare up.

"He was eyeing up your nanny, last time I looked."

They both sighed. "Gone for the afternoon then."

"Darling! Here!"

"It won't be me she's after," said Dallas. "However, I think you've got more important things to sort out. I'll go and see what the old lady wants."

Dallas approached his mother, engaged her in conversation, and slipped an arm around her shoulders in an effort to distract her as Callum followed Gemma.

Gemma fought back the tears as she walked quickly through the house, quiet except for the clatter of plates in the distant kitchen and the banging of doors as waiters walked back and forth. Even the powerful voice of the opera singer and the musicians was muted once she reached the Orangerie. Here she stopped, glanced around, and stepped inside.

Gemma's footfall was quiet on the original clay pavers, either side of which ferns stretched up to the roof, grown tall in the warm, moist air. She stopped at the fountain that lay at the heart of the Orangerie. She could hear nothing but its soothing splash and the distant voice of the singer. Only then did she let the tears fall. She fisted her hands into her dress and stood, gazing up to the glassed dome ceiling and the cobalt blue sky beyond. What the hell was she going to do?

But she had no time to consider as she heard the Orangerie door open and close. The footsteps rang more loudly as they approached. She swiped her thumbs under her eyes in a vain attempt to hide the traces of tears that, no doubt, could be seen all too clearly. It was only moments before Callum appeared around the screen of tall ferns and stopped, as if shocked by what he saw.

"Gemma?"

She cleared her throat. "What? Come to take me back to the reception? Mustn't let our guests see what a complete mess we're making of our lives." She could hear the bitterness and anger in her words but they were too consuming to hide.

He was beside her in a moment. She tried to sidestep around him but he was too quick and slid his arm around her waist. "I'm so sorry, Gemma." She tried to push him away but he didn't weaken his grip.

"For what, exactly? Everything or just the fact you called me 'needy?'" She didn't pause for an answer. "I have no illusions about myself, Callum. But you're wrong. Quite wrong. The only thing I want from you is to care for our child. I've always wanted my independence. It's you who keeps me dependent. You don't want me to work and so, while I'm pregnant, I won't. I've done what I've said I'd do. I've upheld my part of the bargain. Have you?" She pulled away and this time he let her go. "Who was it who took me to the shepherd's cottage all those months ago. Who was it who came to Blackrock and demanded I come with you to Glencoe? And who was it who told me, outside the church, that you cared for me?"

With each sentence, Gemma's voice grew louder, more angry. Callum's grip tightened around her waist but said nothing.

"How *could* you, Callum? How could you act so cold to me in front of your friends and family? And you know what? The worst of it is that I hardly care because the others don't matter. But what *you* say matters to me." She tore his hands from her and pushed past him.

"Gemma! Wait!" He caught up with her and grabbed her hand, holding it tight, so she couldn't run from him. "What do you mean, 'what I say matters to you'? Does it?"

"Of course it does. I thought we'd become friends. Starting with that day in the shepherd's hut. No, we'd become more than friends. I could feel it and so could you. But you backed away again, didn't you? You're the one with the problems that need sorting out. And don't you *dare* come close to me again until they are, because I've been humiliated enough these past weeks. And today was a crowning achievement. Congratulations Callum, you've confirmed everyone's fears, that the scheming woman with the shady past has cornered their precious Callum Mackenzie and won't let him go. Poor Callum, landed with a strange woman and a baby that probably isn't even his."

He gripped her hand more tightly then, his nails digging into her skin. "What do you mean?"

"Well, that's what they're all thinking isn't it? That's what you wonder too, isn't it? If you ever *do* think of me."

"Stop it."

"How would you feel if the baby doesn't look like either of us? A beautiful brown-skinned baby. How would *that* make you feel?"

"Gemma. Stop. I know what you're doing."

"You know nothing about me." Her voice rang around the Orangerie. "Or *my* baby. And you know what? You never will. You'll always have doubts won't you?"

"If I have doubts it'll be harder for me to keep my end of the bargain and to love the child."

"Callum, I just don't care any longer. All I'm hoping from you now is that you'll be able to pretend to care enough to make the child feel secure. Because I don't think you ever have, or ever will love anything in your life. You're a cold, calculating man with no heart."

She winced at her own words, wanted to take them back, but it was too late. Carried away by the pain and anger, the words reflected what, at this moment, she felt, but not what deep down she believed. As she stood hesitating, seeing the shock in his eyes, his fingers released her hand and dropped down to his side. She turned away, hesitated, but he didn't reach out for her. Then she took a step away from him and then another.

"Where are you going?"

She paused but didn't turn to answer because she didn't think she could bear to see the look in his eyes. "Back to our guests. I'm not running away, I'm going to face up to my future, even if you won't."

She walked away, accompanied only by the savage click

of her heels on the clay bricks and an icy determination in her heart. Yes, she hurt deep down and yes, she was trapped in this marriage. But she couldn't run this time. *This* time she'd come out fighting for what she wanted. She stopped by a mirror in the hall and checked her make-up, her gaze shifting to her mouth—set and determined and her eyes, fierce. She was done with trying to please Callum, trying to fit in with his life. She'd build her own world within this one. They'd all have to fit in around her because she wasn't going anywhere.

Cassandra, Gemma decided, was one wonderful woman. Being married to Callum would be a challenge, but getting on with his brother and sister-in-law would be a total joy.

"Lily! Leave the little boy alone!" Cassandra shook her head despairingly as Lily clasped a friend's child around the waist and refused to let him go, despite a desperate wail from the little boy. "She's just like Dallas," Cassandra explained to Gemma as she pried Lily's fingers off the boy. "Single-minded in her pursuit of whatever she wants." Cassandra shot a pleading look at Dallas who grinned, walked over and scooped the little girl up in his arms.

"Must be a family trait," Gemma murmured.

"Oh, yes... Good luck with that." Cassandra glanced over Gemma's shoulder and smiled. "Talk of the devil..."

Gemma followed her gaze. Callum was walking directly towards them, his eyes fixed on her. Gemma turned back to Cassandra and Dallas who exchanged looks.

"Come on, Cassie," Dallas said, "let's introduce James to the joys of children."

"See you later, then, Gemma." Cassandra flashed a

radiant smile, winked at Gemma and was soon hidden by Dallas's warm embrace.

Callum didn't speak but Gemma noticed the jerky swig of beer from the bottle that had replaced the glass of champagne. Callum was nervous. So there was hope. She glanced back at Cassandra and Dallas disappearing across the lawn in search of James and nodded in their direction. "Now, there's a couple in love."

"Really? And you're an expert are you?"

"You don't have to be an expert in something to appreciate it and recognize it in others."

"Interesting. So what are the signs?"

"Of love? Firstly, rather than insulting and ignoring Cassandra, Dallas welcomed her with a kiss and hug and then introduced her to the others in the group."

Callum moved in closer to her, so close she felt the full impact of his animal magnetism stir her body and threaten her mind. But she was too revved up, too angry, to let him take over her senses.

"From your description love sounds a polite, mannered thing. Like there's some kind of set of rules for the whole thing."

She sighed. "It's not a bad idea. Perhaps I should write a book for you, educate you."

"You know all about love, then, do you? Had much experience? You've told me so little about your past, I wouldn't know."

"And when exactly do you think we should have these conversations? While you're making love to me?"

He closed his eyes at the barb. "Of course not."

She shook her head. "There's no other time we're together. *You* make sure of that."

"I do what I have to do."

"Then I suggest you do something different because what you're doing isn't working. I won't put up with it any longer."

His gaze narrowed. "What are you trying to tell me?"

"I'm telling you not to underestimate me, Callum. I've had years of living with a domineering man who could show you a trick or two. And I coped. I learned."

He reacted instantly—his stance more aggressive than seductive now—and fear gripped Gemma's gut. She hadn't meant to say that; she'd meant to keep her past firmly in her past so it didn't threaten her present.

"I thought you said you hardly knew your father?"

She hesitated. But it was too late to backtrack now, too late for lies. Besides, she wanted to force Callum out of his comfort zone. If jealousy, curiosity or whatever would accomplish that, then so be it. She sucked in a deep breath. "Who said I'm talking about my father?"

Her question was met with a stunned silence. "What is it that you're *not* telling me, Gemma?"

She shook her head. "What I'm *telling* you is to make changes, Callum, because I can't go on as we have been."

Her determination to stand her ground faltered under his hard stare. "Did you live with someone before you came here? Tell me."

She had to be firm. "My past has nothing to do with you."

"Sounds like you've been holding back on me. What made you come out here in the first place? All that talk of finding yourself, finding your freedom. You were running from someone, weren't you?"

"Sometimes running from someone is the only thing you can do."

"And is that what you propose to do now? Run away?"

"You know I don't. Things are different now."

"So what is it exactly you want?"

"I want you to accept me into your life, not just at night. Admit your feelings for me." She tiptoed up to him, until her lips nearly touched his ear, until she could feel his breath on her face. "Because I know they're there."

"Do you now?" He looked into her eyes but she couldn't read his thoughts. "And just supposing you're right. Why would I want to admit I had feelings for a woman who keeps her past a mystery and who made it clear from the start that she was only marrying me for the sake of our child?"

She rocked back onto her heels once more as she realized what was really stopping him from opening up to her. "So that's it, you're afraid."

His mouth quirked into a brief smile. "You're quite the psychoanalyst aren't you, Mrs. Mackenzie?"

"Your fear isn't exactly subtle, Mr. Mackenzie."

"Fear has a purpose."

"To stop oneself from hurt. But, Callum... you won't be."

"It's hard."

"Why? Callum, tell me, what happened to freeze your emotions? It was more than Claire's death, wasn't it?" She hated to see the hurt enter his eyes but she had to know.

"She wanted more than I could give."

"What exactly?"

"She was the needy one, not you. And I couldn't give her what she needed. She looked to other people for it and I let her go, believing she'd return. I thought..." He shrugged. "If she needed space I should give it to her and she'd return to me happy."

"Did she?"

"No."

"You can't help everyone. Sometimes it's simply down to them."

"Don't presume to know the situation Gemma, because you haven't any idea what it was like."

She shook her head. "Of course I don't know. But you're going to have to work that through, Callum. Just don't expect to take out your frustrations and anger on me in the meantime." She paused. "Remember," she said softly, "I'm not Claire. Trust me." She brushed her hand lightly down his chest, as she tried to find the strength to tell him what she needed to. She forced herself to meet his direct gaze. "I care for you, Callum. I do. I'm here with you now, I've married you, we're having a baby and I care. What more can I do to make you believe you can trust me?"

Was it the glint of sunlight on his face or did his eyes darken and almost melt as he looked down at her lips? "Give me time," he whispered. He stepped away, his eyes still on hers, as the steeliness crept back into them. He nodded abruptly and awkwardly, thrust his hands in his pockets and walked away.

Gemma's hands crept around her stomach, as the pain of his withdrawal crept through her limbs. For the sake of her baby she had no choice but to give him what he asked.

———

"Where's Gemma gone?" Cassandra called out. Callum turned round to find Cassandra carrying a wriggling, over-tired Lily in her arms. It was late. The sun had dipped below the line of hills and the twilight was deepening.

"I saw her take the path to the look-out a few moments

ago." He'd seen her and was trying to stop himself from following her.

"There's only family left here now, why don't you go after her?" Lily squealed and held out her hands to Callum. "Dallas will keep your mother at bay," Cassandra added.

"Maybe." Instinctively he opened his arms for Lily. His impulse surprised him but, before he could have second thoughts and withdraw his arms, Lily had leaped into them and snuggled against his chest. She immediately stilled, rested her cheek against his chest and began sucking her thumb contentedly.

"You've a knack with kids."

Callum snorted. "Yeah, right."

"No, you have. You over-think things, you doubt yourself too much. Follow your instincts and you won't go wrong —particularly with Gemma, she's lovely."

"I can't. Not yet. I need some time before..."

"Before what? Don't waste time, Callum You've a wonderful future ahead of you. Go grab it."

It was Callum's turn to still. It was as if someone had lifted a blindfold from him, making him see things as they were. Free of his poisonous past, free of the images and words that tainted everything. Perhaps things could be simpler than he'd made them.

"Is that how you see things? So straightforward"

She nodded, amused. "It's how they are." Lily's eyelids began to droop, despite her best efforts to keep awake. Callum stroked his finger down her soft cheek and swallowed hard. "Come here," Cassandra smiled. "Let me take Lily. It's time she was in bed."

Callum gently handed Lily to Cassandra. Lily didn't awake, simply nestled into her mother's arms with a contented wriggle.

Cassandra placed a gentle hand on his arm. "Go see Gemma. Make it right. There's nothing that time will do for you, that you can't do for yourself. Now."

He nodded. "How did Dallas deserve such a wise woman as yourself?"

She grinned. "He didn't. He just got lucky."

Callum watched Cassandra walk back to the house before turning his gaze up to the look-out, above the house. He could just make out Gemma's white dress, glowing like a beacon in the dusk.

Gemma looked out across the lights that dotted the plains to the faint red glow that still lit the western horizon.

It was utterly beautiful and she felt totally exhausted. The future was all before her but she had no idea what it would bring. She pushed her hands through her hair, twisting it off her neck to allow the balmy night breeze to cool her. Then she heard a twig snap. She didn't turn around. She knew who it would be. "Callum... is it over yet?"

He didn't reply immediately, as if trying to figure out what she meant. "The reception? Yes, most people have gone. Cassandra's putting the kids to bed and Dallas is trying to distract mother from locating James."

She turned to him. He stood on the fringe of the native bush, several feet away from her, only his dark silhouette and the light of his eyes and shirt visible in the dusk. "That will take some doing."

"Yep." Callum moved beside her. "But if anyone can do it, Dallas can."

"You think a lot of Dallas, don't you?"

"He's a tough man but he's always been there for me."

He shrugged. "Always been there for everyone. But now he's got Cassandra, we're seeing a different side to him. One we didn't even know existed."

"A softer side?"

Callum snorted. "That'll be the day. But, yeah, I guess you're right. He's happy. That much is obvious."

"And are you happy, Callum?"

He didn't meet her gaze, but continued to look out into the dark night. "Happier than I've a right to be."

"You are?"

"Gemma," he reached for her hand but didn't look at her. "I was wrong."

A cold chill ran through her body. Was he going to reject her here and now, on their wedding day? She swallowed drily. "About?"

He must have sensed her fear because he turned to her, a soft smile playing on his lips. "About needing time." He pulled her closer to him, slipped his hand under her chin and lifted her face until her lips touched his. His body and mouth were hot against hers, filling her with hope. Slowly he withdrew, put his arm around her and pulled her to his side until she was nestled into his body. They looked out across the wide valley to the violet-gray haze of the hills beyond and listened to the soft calls of nocturnal birds that mingled with the ebb and flow of classical music and the distant murmur and laughter of the few remaining guests. "I'm beginning to believe I won't need as much time as I thought."

She closed her eyes with happiness at his words and at the strength of his body holding hers. "Good." It was too plain a word to convey her feelings, but she was scared she'd break down if she said any more. She cleared her throat.

"All I've ever wanted is here." Callum paused for a long

time but Gemma didn't speak. "For a long time all I wanted was this land." Gemma followed his gaze out across Glencoe and beyond to where Blackrock land lay. "And now, between us, we have it all."

Gemma frowned, as a creeping chill began a slow, inexorable climb up her body. She tried to form the right words but they dried on her lips. "Callum, I..."

"Let me finish. I need to say this. It used to be all about the land but, since I met you, I realized the land wasn't enough—"

Gemma held up her hand and pressed her fingers to his lips. "Callum, I need to tell you something." She licked her lips nervously. "Blackrock, it isn't exactly mine. I don't own it."

"What do you mean? Of course you do."

"No. I don't own it. It belongs to a friend of mine."

"What the hell are you talking about?" His words were ejected in distinct syllables like bullets.

His anger sparked a dull thudding in her temples. "I had to get out of London. It's complicated to explain."

"I'm sure it is. Seems everything's too complicated to explain, so you lie. Have you told me anything that's true? All that sob story about your past, is any of that true?"

"Of course it is." She paused. "Everything's true, except for the fact I inherited Blackrock. I didn't. It's my friend's place and she still owns it. Just has no interest in it. She said I can stay as long as I like. She can't sell it, there's some kind of legal caveat thingy on it. So she reckoned I may as well make use of it."

"So convenient."

"It was."

"For you. But not for me."

She shook her head. "I don't understand. What difference does it make?"

"All the difference in the world. I've been working through the courts for years, trying to get hold of Blackrock. My grandfather gambled it away. I want it back. Glencoe isn't complete without it."

The pain of having to tell him her secret, admit that she'd lied to him, suddenly gave way to the pain of understanding why he'd really married her. "I know you never wanted me but I thought, truly thought, you wanted our child. But you didn't, did you? It was the land you wanted. God," she closed her eyes, trying to keep in the hurt, "I've been so stupid."

"The truth? I wanted both. I didn't have to make a choice."

She shook her head, half smiling at the hard, unadorned truth that was so like Callum.

"And now?" He didn't speak. She pulled off the wedding ring and tossed it to him. He caught it and folded his fingers around it. "Keep it. I don't want it. I guess you can say the deal's off. I haven't kept my end of the bargain, so I'll leave."

"I want my child."

"Maybe. But you want the land more." She turned and walked away.

"Where are you going?"

"To the only thing I have left. My house."

"It's not yours."

"I'll be living there from now on, even if I don't own it."

Gemma half stumbled down the dusty path, back to the house. She had to leave, had to get out of there, away from Callum. Everything now made perfect sense. All Callum had ever wanted was the land and an heir to leave it to. He'd thought he'd got both in her, but he'd get neither.

Gemma drove away unnoticed by the few remaining people who continued to drink on the verandah of Glencoe. She drove the straight road without daring to think or feel, postponing the moment until she was alone.

By the time she reached Blackrock, night had fallen and the darkness around the house was complete. She switched off the engine and let the dust subside for a moment before stepping out into the night. Immediately her nostrils flared at the faint smell of cigarette smoke. She shrugged—must be on her clothes from the reception—and walked up the steps to the front door.

She closed her eyes. Key. Damn. She'd been in such a state she hadn't brought the key with her. She tried the handle but it was locked, just as she thought. Then she remembered the faulty lock on the sash window of her bedroom. She picked up a stool from the shed and walked carefully around the house, feeling the wall as she went. When she reached her bedroom, she stretched out, gripped the edge of the window frame and lifted the window high. That smell again. Strange. It seemed stronger here. She breathed in deeply. Much stronger.

She sat on the frame, swung over her feet and dropped down onto the wooden floorboards of her bedroom with a thud. She fumbled her way across to the lamp and switched it on.

"Gemma!" She turned to see Paul leaning against the door, arms crossed. "Kind of you to save me the trouble of gate-crashing your wedding."

---

# CHAPTER TEN

Gemma couldn't move. Her mouth dried and she opened it to scream but no sound came. There was no one to hear it anyway. She was quite alone with a man who was as unpredictable as he was dangerous. Beyond the circle of lamplight, his eyes, which she knew to be as blue as Callum's, were as black as midnight and fixed on hers. He betrayed no emotion as he continued to watch her with riveting focus that made her forget about everything else. It had been that same intensity that had first drawn her to him, an intensity she'd mistaken for love. She'd forgotten the effect it had always had on her. It stirred in her such a complex blend of fear, attraction and sadness that she felt light-headed.

A slow smile settled on his handsome face. He was aware of her response. He knew her too well. She should hate him. She *did* hate him, she told herself. He pushed himself away from the wall and walked over to her. Her heart pounded heavily, trying to give life to her limbs that refused to move. Still, she couldn't take her eyes off him, the full force of memory slamming into her, transporting her back to her past life.

He stopped in front of her. He was as tall as Callum but not as big-boned. But she knew his body, knew the taut muscles and its wiry strength. It had, at one and the same time, attracted her and frightened her. She forced herself to look down, focusing on the cross at his neck, a symbol so at odds with his lack of morals that she'd never been able to understand how he could reconcile his faith with how he lived his life.

"I was *joking*, Gemma. I know it couldn't be your wedding, no matter what I've been told." He tilted her chin firmly up so she was forced to look into those cold, cold eyes once more. "I've come to take you home." She trembled at his touch. She closed her eyes before they betrayed the ambiguity it sparked. She shook her head, still unable to speak. "Come on," he said softly. "Time to go." He glanced around her home with a faint smile. "I don't want you in this place a moment longer. It's a wreck."

She shook her head again. "It's my home." She tried to step away but his hand tightened on her wrist.

"It's Sarah's home, not yours." His mouth curled upward in a cruel smile that had never been aimed at her before. He pinched her chin between his fingers, too hard. "Not yours," he repeated. He blinked slowly, as if for control. His eyes turned blank once more and he stepped away.

Out from under the control of his eyes, Gemma found her voice and her strength. "I'm not leaving, Paul, *you* are."

He turned to face her. "Not without you." His voice was harsh and his lips had tightened into a straight line, losing the initial softness that had almost made her forget what he was really like. Suddenly she remembered everything. A thousand memories flooded into her mind. She had to get him away, make him leave before he inflicted on her the kind of deliberate, cold cruelty she'd seen him make others suffer. But she knew she couldn't do it by force. She had to make him see.

"No. I left you, Paul. I left because I couldn't live with you any longer."

The smile dropped. "No, you were playing games. You wanted me to find you."

She swallowed and drew in a jerky breath. "No. I left without a word because I knew you wouldn't let me leave you."

He must have heard the fear in her voice, because he stepped towards her, too close, his head cocked to one side. "Why would you want to leave me? I gave you everything."

"I didn't want everything. I wanted my freedom."

He smiled as if the notion was ridiculous. "Ah, there you have me. There's a limit to my indulgence, Princess." He looked around the room, at the scanty furniture, the brightly painted walls, uneven under the original scrim covering. "So, this is what freedom brings."

"It's what I want. I don't expect you to understand."

"Then let's stop talking about it. We'll be back in London by tomorrow."

"No."

He shook his head. "You were clever, I'll give you that. I'd never have thought to look for you here if Sarah hadn't slipped up."

"She's okay, isn't she?"

He shrugged. "No idea. She mentioned to a friend that she knew you were okay. So I had her apartment searched and her phone told me everything I needed to know. She supplied the rest of the details. In what state my men left her, I've no idea. Not interested."

"No..." Gemma groaned. She felt sick to her stomach. Sarah had put herself on the line to help her out, and she'd ended up paying. But what price?

"You were clever though," Paul continued. "Because I had no idea you two were such good friends."

"We kept it quiet." She drew a deep breath. She knew what he was capable of. But she had no choice because she knew he'd never believe it if he didn't hear it from her. "I don't love you, Paul. I don't want to be with you."

He shook his head, his expression revealing only confidence. Ambiguity and confusion weren't things Paul suffered from. "Silly girl." He drew in a deep breath and lifted his chin as if seeking air. He walked away from her, raised the second sash window and flicked out a still-lighted cigarette. "It's quiet here, no-one around for miles. No-one to see anything, no-one to hear anything."

"It won't be for long. I have...friends arriving soon."

He turned back to her and she couldn't see his face against the last of the evening light. "Friends," he repeated. "And what kind of friends are these, hey, Gemma?" He came close to her and she felt the quickened breath of anger against her cheek. Through years of experience, she didn't move. "I received reports. I ignored them, told them they must have been following the wrong woman. My Princess wouldn't sleep with another man. She's mine. And she knows that."

A shiver ran down her spine. She swallowed. "I'm not yours, Paul."

He frowned and swiped his finger down the side of her face. "Yes, you are. Perhaps you've forgotten. Perhaps I need to remind you."

She shook her head, fear beginning to take its stifling hold of every part of her. "No..."

He smiled as if she hadn't spoken. "Do you remember when we first met?" His hand barely touched her face, so gentle was his touch. "You were so sweet and innocent. I loved that. You opened up like a flower for me. And I thought, she's special. And I need to look after her in a special way, need to wrap her in cotton wool so nothing can hurt her." She closed her eyes against the soft but deadly touch of his hand. "Don't tell me you thought differently because I know you didn't."

"Not then."

"And not now." He walked around her, a full circle before facing her once more. "These reports... They're not true, are they? Tell me..."

She shook her head, unable to utter a word, frozen by fear.

In those moments of unspoken communication, she saw his expression change from tenderness to anger. He lifted his hand to her neck, as if to caress it but, instead, ripped her jacket open. The buttons fell off and spun, rolling along the wooden floor. Her first instinct was to slip her hands in front of her stomach. But it was too late. Slowly, she forced herself to stand with her hands at each side, her rounded stomach in full evidence. His ice-blue eyes sparked with fire. What the hell was he going to do?

---

"For Christ's sake, Callum, go after her." Dallas could barely keep his short temper in check. "It's your wedding day and you screwed up."

Callum paced away from his two brothers, unable to look into their faces, full of accusation.

"Just do it," James added. "You've always been pig-headed and stubborn, but this is ridiculous."

"Why the hell should I? If she lied about owning Black-rock, what else did she lie about? How can I ever trust her again?"

"What the hell does one lie matter?"

"It matters to me."

"You can live without Blackrock. What's so important about it?"

Callum turned to Dallas. "It's all good for you, isn't it? The golden boy who earned the cash to keep everything together after Dad stuffed up."

"Not all good, Callum, believe me. I had responsibilities and—"

"And so do I. You did what you had to do for the family, for us, and that's what I want, too."

"Now, if we could just talk about my expertise for a moment," James interrupted. "*Women*. You wanted Gemma. You didn't marry her for the land. I don't believe that for one minute."

Callum looked from one brother to the other. It was time for the truth. "No, I didn't. Believe it or not, I'm not angry because of losing Blackrock, it's more than that. It's about trust. Without trust, what is there?"

"Love. That's what," said Dallas. "You love Gemma. It shows in everything you do. You love her and you're about to throw away a lifetime's happiness because of a lie over a piece of land?"

Callum didn't turn back to face them, but squeezed his eyes tight shut as the truth hit him. "Do you think she'll come back?"

"I think a lot of groveling is in order."

Callum shook his head and opened his eyes. "No. She'll be back. She'll realize how stupidly stubborn she's being. I'll wait for her to come."

Both James and Dallas groaned and shook their heads. Callum ignored them, poured himself a whisky and made himself comfortable on the leather sofa. He'd wait. She'd come.

---

When Paul's gaze lifted from her stomach there was hate in his eyes. The old Paul had gone. He ground his teeth.

"Did he force himself on you?"

She bit her lip. She was scared of him, of what he could do, but not to her. He'd never been violent with her. But now? "No, he didn't, Paul. He *didn't*. It wasn't like that."

He blew out a deep breath. "You never lied to me in the past. What are you hiding now?"

"I'm telling you the truth."

He shook his head and paced across the room. "So this Callum Mackenzie. Local hot shot is he?"

Should she make Callum less than he was to stop Paul's jealousy? But one look at Paul made her realize it was too late. And, if he knew how powerful the Mackenzies were, it might make him think twice. "Yes, he is. His family owns much of the land and wealth around here." She paused. "They have wide networks."

He pushed himself off the wall and approached her. "All sounds very proper to me. And 'very proper' doesn't worry me. There are much more effective ways of doing business. So, tell me about him."

"What do you want to know?"

"Why is he at Glencoe and you, here?"

"I'm... just here to pick up some stuff."

"So, the pregnant bit of the rumor wasn't wrong. What about the wedding part? They told me there was a big Mackenzie wedding at Glencoe. They told me it was your wedding. Again, I dismissed it, I didn't believe them. I want to hear it from you. Tell me, Gemma, whose wedding was it?"

"Mine." The word was barely more than a pressing together of her lips.

He shook his head, his lips curling with distaste. His face was flushed with anger as he paced the room, looking anywhere but at her. Suddenly he strode up to the wall and punched it hard. His fist went right through the flimsy wall, revealing the wooden battens behind. He turned back to her as if nothing had happened and strode over to her, his face, dipped to one side, staring her straight in the eye.

"Was it marriage you wanted? You should have told me. We could have married."

She shook her head. She couldn't speak even if she wanted to. Fear had her gripped in its icy control.

"So you only married him for the baby. How touching, how traditional. But you're here now." He brushed a strand of her hair off her cheek. "You must have realized you'd made a mistake."

She shook her head again.

"Then why are you both in separate places? This Mackenzie man in Glencoe and you, here. Strange on your wedding day." She didn't answer. "Did he hurt you, Gemma?"

She shook her head, suddenly realizing where the conversation was leading. "No."

"He did, didn't he?"

Terror seized her. It wasn't just about her anymore. It was about what Paul and his men might do to Callum. She had to get him far away from here.

"I'll pack my bag, Paul, I'll come with you."

"No. We're not going anywhere before I teach Callum Mackenzie a lesson." He glanced at his watch. "Best he come to us. Ring him. Tell him to come. I'll get the truth from him."

She shook her head. No way in this world was she bringing Callum here. Paul would kill him. There'd been enough rumors, enough newspaper headlines, to make her realize exactly how deep his underground criminal network went in London. *And* the extent of the violence.

He pulled out his phone. "Second thoughts, he'll know what awaits him if you phone. I always like an element of surprise." She shivered. "I'm told Glencoe isn't so far away from here. Not so far away that he won't see smoke rising. I'll light a fire." He grinned, a cold, travesty of a smile. "I was always good at lighting fires."

"We have no wood."

"Oh, I think we do." He looked pointedly at the wood paneling and at the timber construction his fist had exposed. She closed her eyes. *Not the house.* "He should be able to see the smoke from where he is. We'll smoke him out, like a rat."

---

"Is that smoke?" Callum rose from his chair and pushed open the window, narrowed his eyes, trying to distinguish the shifting dark clouds from the darker plume that was drifting upwards.

Dallas and James came up behind him.

"Looks like it," Dallas replied, peering into the distance. "What the hell?"

"Fire." James said. "At Blackrock. Looks like Gemma's in trouble."

Callum picked up a cell phone and tossed it to Dallas as all three of them ran out into the night.

"Call emergency services. They won't get there for half an hour. We're Gemma's only chance."

As the Range Rover roared off into the night, the smoke became clearer as it billowed up, a stain of dark gray on the indigo sky. Fear gripped Callum, steely and visceral, but he focused on driving over the rough ground that provided a shortcut to Blackrock. The car lurched forward as it flew over boulders and skidded, wheels spinning and screeching, on the dusty ground. As he topped a ridge he saw what he knew in his heart already. Flames were licking out of the rear bedroom window, it would be an inferno in minutes only. He slammed his foot on the accelerator and they roared down the hill towards the burning building.

He leaped out of the car and his blood turned to ice as he heard a scream.

"You take the front," He yelled to Dallas and James as he tore round the back of the house to where the scream had come from—Gemma's bedroom. The heat and smoke hit him like a wall and he came to an abrupt halt. The house was entirely made of wood and would be history in minutes. He backtracked and launched himself into the French window that Gemma had cracked as she'd left the house all those weeks ago. Glass and wood splintered and smoke rushed to meet the air. Coughing, he covered his face with his arm and looked quickly around. Her bedroom was ablaze and there was nothing to see, except the billowing black, acrid smoke that made his eyes stream and seeped into his lungs. Then he heard another scream, this time from outside.

As soon as he leaped back through the window he'd smashed, flames engulfed the house. He ran around the front in time to see a tall man he'd never seen before, his back to him and his arm tightly around Gemma, too tight around her stomach. Blind fury gripped Callum as he came up behind the stranger. He grabbed both arms and twisted them behind him, releasing Gemma, who James promptly grabbed and pulled to one side. Callum now had a clear shot at the off-balance stranger and delivered a right hook straight to his chin. The stranger reeled back and landed on the dusty ground.

Callum stood, panting over him, waiting for him to move, *wanting* him to move so he could vent the uncontrollable rage that pounded through every vein. But the man barely shook his head, tried to sit up and then dropped his head again. The white light that had invaded Callum's brain slowly receded. The man was obviously concussed and Callum looked away, searching for Gemma.

He didn't see her at first. Just heard Dallas and James yelling to each other as they connected up the hose and pointed it at the fire. Smoke billowed out of the house but the fire continued to burn. The hose wasn't powerful enough so the two men focused on soaking the area around the house to stop the spread of fire, getting it under control just as the fire siren sounded in the distance.

Callum groped forward through the smoke and suddenly heard her cough as she moved away from the heat of the flames and thick smoke that filled the air.

He strode over to her. "You okay?"

"I think so." She was looking down at the stranger who

still lay, semi-conscious on the ground. "We're safe now, aren't we?" She looked up with scared and trusting eyes.

"Yes. He's not going anywhere in a hurry."

"And the fire?"

"Under control." He gestured to his brothers. "They know what to do. We grew up out here, remember." He held her face gently in his hands and brushed the streaky soot from her cheeks. "You sure you're okay?"

She nodded. "He didn't hurt me." She tilted her head to one side as she held his gaze and slid her hand around his cheek. "I'm okay. *Really*. He just scared the living daylights out of me." She tried to smile, tried to reassure but it would take more than a watery smile to banish the memory imprinted on Callum's mind, of Gemma, trapped by the arms of this stranger.

"What was he after? Money? Why the hell would he want to hurt you, someone he didn't know?"

A pained look came over Gemma's face, but before she could answer, a shout from Dallas roused them both.

"Get in the car," Callum insisted. "Lock it and stay there. I'm going to help Dallas and James."

He waited only to make sure Gemma had done as he wanted before he joined his brothers, while still keeping an eye on the prostrate figure. It was too late to save the house but they managed to contain the fire, and the surrounding trees and grass escaped the inferno. It was only minutes before the fire truck arrived and took over.

The three men, blackened, exhausted and coughing moved back to the stranger who was now standing, shaking his head and swaying. Gemma joined them.

He focused unsteadily on her and tried to walk towards her but James grabbed the man's arms and drew them up his back. "You're not going anywhere."

"Who the hell are you?" Callum asked, walking up to the stranger until they were practically nose to nose.

The man hadn't shifted his gaze from Gemma. "Are you going to tell them, Princess?"

Callum turned slowly to Gemma, a sickening chill sinking into his gut. "Gemma?" he gasped. No one would have heard above the noise of the fire truck and the men who still worked on soaking the dying embers of the house.

"No answer, Gemma?" the man asked. "Perhaps I should tell them." He spat blood onto the blackened ground and then looked at Callum with cold, murderous eyes. "She's my lover, my partner, my girlfriend. Whatever else you want to call her."

Callum flexed his fist ready to launch it once more into the man's face when he felt a gentle touch on his arm. "No don't, Callum. Let me explain."

Callum couldn't bring himself to look at Gemma. He kept his eyes on the man. "Go on. I'm listening."

"This is Paul. My ex. From London."

Callum closed his eyes briefly as jealousy slammed into him with a force he felt physically. "Ex. So not 'lover.'"

"No. Not."

Callum watched as Paul's eyes focused, not angrily, but puzzled, on Gemma. He shook his head. "Why deny it, Princess? You've made a mistake and now you're coming home, with me."

Gemma face was white with shock. She shook her head. But Callum hadn't a clue whether the gesture was meant for him or for the stranger.

"Just tell me, Gemma, what the hell's going on?"

"Paul won't be alone, Callum. He'll have arranged for his men to arrive soon."

"If he had other people in New Zealand, they'd be here, now, with him. Wouldn't they?" He turned to Paul.

Paul nodded slowly. "I decided to come alone to get Gemma back. My mistake."

"The police are on their way." Dallas pocketed his cell phone.

"Gemma! For God's sake what are you playing at? It's time to go home. With me."

"Can't you see, Paul? It's over. I'm pregnant, married to Callum. My future's here."

Paul shook his head, disbelieving. "It's not over. You're wrong."

James yanked Paul away from Callum while Dallas stepped between them.

"Callum, why don't you take Gemma home and James and I will look after our visitor." Callum knew what Dallas was doing. Dallas was afraid Callum would hit Paul and keep on hitting him. That he wouldn't be able to stop. And he was right. Callum nodded to Dallas and put his arm around Gemma and walked towards the car without a further word.

But Gemma turned back to James. "Where are you taking him?" Gemma's soft voice cut through the thick smoky atmosphere.

"To let the cops deal with him."

"It's not over, Gemma," Paul whispered.

Callum pulled Gemma away.

"She'll leave you," Paul called to Callum's back as he and Gemma walked away. "Don't think she won't. She came from nowhere. She'll disappear there again. You can't trust her."

Dallas was called over by the fire crew and Paul took the opportunity to suddenly swing an accurate, sharp punch at James's face, taking him by surprise, followed by a swift kick to his groin. James doubled over, releasing Paul from his grip and, before Dallas or Callum could reach Paul, he'd jumped into his car and roared off, on to the road, towards town. Dallas jumped into his car and sped off close behind.

James pulled out his cell phone. "I'll have people waiting for him in Shelter Springs. He won't get far."

The three of them watched the smoldering mess that was all that was left of Blackrock homestead.

"Nothing left," Callum murmured.

"And you know what that means," James added. "The caveat's gone and the land can be sold."

Callum shook his head. He couldn't even think about that now. He was hurting in every fiber of his body. Not because of the smoke inhalation, not because of the minor burns on his hands, but because Gemma hadn't trusted him with the truth and he'd not been there to protect her. Yet again, he'd failed to protect the woman he loved.

He closed his eyes as the last thought jumped, fully formed, into his head. *He loved.* Of course he loved her but he'd been too damned scared to admit it. "Come on, I'll take you home."

"Home?" She shook her head. "My home's gone."

"Glencoe, I mean."

They exchanged silent looks as she climbed into the car and slumped back against the seat, exhausted. There were so many things to say. But they could wait. He had to get her home and safe first.

A dull red glow still lingered in the sky behind them as they drove back to Glencoe.

"So... as James said, now there's no house, there's no caveat. You can buy the land from Sarah. You'll get the land because of me, just not quite how you expected to. If this had happened yesterday, you wouldn't have married me."

"I would still have married you."

Her brows knitted together in angry confusion. "Why the hell would you want to do that? You can have access to your child without marriage, you can get the land you so wanted. What else would marriage give you?"

He glanced at her. "You."

She turned away abruptly. "Me." There was a long pause. "That's right. That way you have control. Just like..."

Before Callum could respond, his phone rang.

"It's me," Dallas's voice came over the speaker. "Is this on speaker?"

"Yep," Callum replied.

"Then take it off."

Callum frowned and brought the phone to his ear. He listened to Dallas's brief words and clicked off the phone.

"What was that about?"

Callum hesitated. "It's Paul."

"What about him?" Callum hated the concern in her voice.

"Dallas found a car in the river—Paul's car. It failed to take the horseshoe bend. The police are there now and they can't find any trace of him."

Gemma groaned and pulled her hands up around her face and curled into the seat, away from him.


Gemma felt numb as she stepped out of the car in front of Glencoe, now deserted of visitors. She followed Callum into the library and sat down gratefully. Soot streaked his face, his eyes were red from smoke and his mouth was grim.

"Why didn't you tell me about him?"

"I couldn't. He was my past, a past I was running from and was terrified would catch up with me." She shook her head. "I couldn't tell anyone."

"You didn't trust me."

"I was scared. I didn't trust anyone to know about him. I'd tried to leave him before but my plans had always been blown by so-called friends. I couldn't trust anyone."

"You could have trusted me."

"I didn't know that to start with and by the time I realized I could, it seemed too late to tell you. I rationalized it by saying that it wasn't your business, it was mine. I was wrong."

"Tell me now."

"He wasn't an easy man to leave. He loved me in his own way. I had to leave everything behind and tell no one where I was going. He wouldn't let me go anywhere without his knowing, he didn't want me to wear anything other than what he chose, I couldn't talk to anyone he didn't approve of. And God forbid if someone chatted me up. I'd never see them again. And then I started to hear how he made his money. I began to see where his tight-knit group of friends and relatives fitted into the scene. People came to them with grievances and they fixed them. I suddenly discovered I was locked into a strait jacket in the center of a gang of criminals."

"And so you found yourself staring at a map in the middle of New Zealand one day."

She nodded. They sat in silence as Maria walked in with a tray of hot drinks and food. Maria began to speak but Callum silenced her with a look. The door clicked shut after Maria left.

"It's over now, Gemma." He couldn't read the expression in her eyes.

"Yes, it is."

"You and Paul, it's over. Finished."

"No, Callum. It's you and I who have no future."

"What?"

She saw the shock in his eyes. He didn't understand her at all.

"I'm sorry. I'm grateful for what you did with Paul, back there, I really am. But don't you see? What you and your brothers did was exactly like Paul and his gang would have done. Bowled on in, thrown a few punches and sorted things out and then carried off the woman." She stood up wearily. Her legs felt like lead, her heart felt even heavier. "I can't deal with that. I can't live my life like that. It's not me. I don't want it. You're all so controlling and I don't want to be controlled. Why can't you understand that?"

"Controlling? It's just..." He shrugged. She could see that he found it difficult to understand what she was saying because how he'd behaved was second nature to him. "Just sorting out a situation. What did you want me to do? Say, 'Hi Paul, how's it going? Want to manhandle my wife, that's fine, go ahead.'"

"No of course not." She shook her head in confusion. "No. I'm grateful. Really. You got me out of a bad situation. But I can't stand being pushed and pulled about like some kind of helpless pawn. I need space to be myself."

He shook his head. "I don't understand."

"No. I know you don't. And until you can understand, we have no future." She walked over to the door.

"Where are you going?"

"Into Shelter Springs. I'll go to Rebecca's. She'll put me up."

"Stay. At least tonight. Stay here, in your room. We can talk."

"And go round and round? No, I've got to move on, Callum."

"Not with my child."

"Well," she smiled sadly. "I can't very well leave him behind, can I?"

"Stay."

She shook her head.

"I'll drive you there."

"I've asked Morgan."

Callum stepped back. "You've got it all worked out."

"No, the only thing I've worked out is what I don't want." She walked away, her heart breaking with every step but it would be more than her heart she'd be breaking if she stayed, it would be her spirit. "I'll be in touch."

"Gemma. Come back to me. Soon. I'll be waiting."

# CHAPTER ELEVEN

Winter had arrived early and only a few russet leaves still clung to the trees that lined the lakefront road. Callum had let weeks pass into months while he waited for Gemma to heal and to understand. But the waiting hadn't worked and she still hadn't returned to Glencoe.

He lifted the collar of his coat to keep out the chill wind that blew down from the mountains and stippled the surface of the glacial green lake. He patted his jacket, searching for the outline of the sheaf of papers tucked in his inside pocket. Satisfied, he looked across at The Lakehouse Café. The afternoon light was waning and electric light spilled out into the gloom from its tall windows. Laughter and music wafted across to him on the chill breeze. The passenger door clunked shut and James joined him and together they walked across the car-lined street.

James raised his eyebrows. "Ready to face your wife?"

"I've been ready for a while."

"Then you should have made a move before now. Have you spoken to her at all?"

"A little. We talked about her friend, Sarah, who's okay. But mainly about McCarthy—her ex."

James nodded grimly. "Sounds like he's gone to ground in the UK."

"He'll never be allowed back into New Zealand. He'd be arrested at the border if he tried."

"Must have been some comfort to Gemma."

"Must have been. Don't know. We didn't talk much."

"I can't see there's much to say. I can't understand why you didn't do your usual macho display, go round there and carry her off."

They walked up the steps to the café. "Yeah, right. That would have frightened her off for sure. No, I've been waiting for her to make the first move. It's up to her."

James opened the door. "Good luck. If you need any tips, just ask."

Callum ignored James's wide grin and didn't bother to reply. He grabbed a drink from a passing waiter and made his way through the crowds, looking for Gemma. Suddenly a group of people moved out of the way and Gemma came into view. She was resting on a stool, talking animatedly to a group of people who were studying one of her many paintings on display around the café.

James came and stood beside him as Rebecca, Gemma's friend, passed by. Callum greeted her and James twisted round, following Rebecca with his eyes as she walked away.

James whistled under his breath, turned back to Callum and grinned.

"Don't go there, James, not unless you want Morgan on your back."

"Why?" James leaned against a wall and sipped his red wine. "Are they an item?"

"Not yet, but not through want of trying on Morgan's part. The lovely Rebecca has her mind on the stars."

"She works at the observatory, you said?"

"She's an astronomer doing research on something that fries my brain just thinking about it."

"That's because you're a practical man, whereas I, dear brother, understand all about women with stars in their eyes. In fact, I like to put them there in the first place. The lovely Rebecca's probably just waiting for me to make my move."

Callum shook his head. Anyone who didn't know James's legendary love life might have thought him to be conceited. He probably was, but not without reason. "So are you going to ask Rebecca out?"

James smiled. "What a quaint, old-fashioned idea. So typical of you, Callum. But, no. No time to do her justice. I'm due back at Napa Valley next week." He looked around at Gemma's paintings. "She's a good artist."

"She's a great artist." Callum corrected, his eyes not shifting from Gemma.

"Looks like her separation from you has sparked her creativity."

Irritated, Callum swigged back his beer. "She painted most of them before our wedding. It was Lizzi, the café manager who persuaded her she should put on an exhibition."

"Gemma looks pretty happy." It was exactly what Callum was thinking. It was exactly what Callum had been afraid of. "Any chance of you two getting back together?"

"There's always a chance."

"So, tell me again why you haven't seen her before now," James continued. He obviously wasn't going to let it go.

"I reckon she needed some time to get her head around everything that happened."

"But she invited you here today for her exhibition." James sipped his wine. "That's a good sign."

Callum shrugged. He had no idea what kind of sign it was. He just knew it was an opportunity to give her the papers.

He continued to watch Gemma, her hair twisted up and caught in an elegant knot, her loose dress flowing over her rounded body. He started to say something to James but discovered his younger brother flirting with the waitress. Then Gemma turned, her polite smile relaxing into a warm smile of welcome as it rested on Callum. She raised her eyebrows in invitation. It was all Callum needed. He placed his drink on the table and walked over to her.

She stretched out her hand and squeezed his. He bent down and kissed her on the cheek. "You look wonderful, Gemma."

"I feel good. Looking forward to the little one making an appearance, though."

"No names yet? You wanted Violet Rose, if I remember rightly."

She grinned. "And you wanted Joan. We never did have that discussion, did we?"

"No." There was a long pause. Words swam into Callum's head only to float out again. He'd thought about what he should say for weeks, but now the words had vanished. Just looking at her here, so self-possessed, surrounded by friends, her red hair gleaming under the bright lights, her eyes shining and full of life, she was a stranger to him. Callum sucked in a deep breath and felt inside his jacket for the papers. But, before he could produce them there was a shout and Gemma was distracted.

"Gemma! Over here. The photographers want a shot of you for one of the national papers."

Gemma looked at Callum questioningly.

"You go." The smile vanished from her face in an instant and Callum reached out to hold her back but his gesture was too late and Gemma was soon lost amidst a throng of art-lovers, locals and reporters. Callum took a step back out of the way. He wasn't wanted here. Gemma was his wife in name only. Neither of them had made steps to formally separate but he could see she'd made a new life for herself and he wasn't a part of it.

He was happy for her. He was. He turned around and walked out of the café.

It was ridiculous, but it hurt him to see her so happy, surrounded by people he didn't even know. She'd moved away from him. There was nothing more he could give her. He had to face the hurt that he'd tried to protect himself from for so long.

Out by the lake, the cool air was misting above the grass. He tugged open his collar, wanting the crisp air on his skin, wanting to feel something other than the pain of watching the woman he loved move further and further away from him.

He looked out across to the mountains until his eyes burned with the brightness of their snow-capped peaks capturing the last of the sunlight. Eventually he had to look away and he rubbed his watering eyes.

"Callum?"

He stood stock still. He was hearing things now. He sighed and shook his head, trying to rid it of the lingering image and sounds of Gemma.

"Callum." He closed his eyes at her light touch and then swung round to face her.

Gemma was out of breath. It wasn't just the exercise—although God knew, she'd done little enough over the past few months except paint at her easel in Rebecca's cottage—it was also fear. She'd barely turned her back on Callum before he'd gone. "You disappeared in a rush. I've been looking for you."

Callum looked down at his feet and then away, over her shoulder. It seemed he didn't want to face her. "You were busy, so I thought it best if I leave."

Gemma swallowed her fears. "So... you just came out of politeness, then."

He shrugged noncommittally. "You invited me. I had nothing else on tonight."

She nodded and kept on nodding like some crazy nodding toy. It was her turn to look away. She sighed sharply. "Right. Well. Don't let me keep you. I guess things have changed over the past few months." *I guess you don't want me any more.* That was what she wanted to say but it would be too humiliating to hear him agree.

"Yes."

"For me, too." She chewed her lip. She waited but he didn't go. She lifted her chin defiantly. She wouldn't be the first one to leave this time. "The exhibition... did you like it?"

"You're a good artist."

She shrugged and managed a brief smile. "Thanks. It's strange putting my works out in the public for all to see. But..." She tailed off and shrugged nervously once more. "It seemed the right time to do it."

"Before the baby."

"Yes." She held his blue gaze for the first time. "Before the baby."

"How have you been keeping?"

Was it her imagination or was his gaze warmer now? "Fine. As I'm sure Dr Cooper's told you."

Callum frowned. "He said that you'd told him it was okay to share information with me. I assumed..."

"Yes, sure. That's fine. I've got nothing to hide." Her smiled faded. "Not any more, anyway." Another pause. "So, what's the news from Glencoe?"

He cleared his throat. "I've bought Blackrock."

"I thought you would. You know, I never did under-stand the whole story about the caveat."

"Family feud, generations ago. My grandfather lost the land in a gambling game and Sarah's ancestor was deter-mined our family wouldn't be able to buy it back again in several lifetimes. Hence the caveat that the land could only be sold if there was no house on it."

"Why didn't they renovate it, keep it going then?"

He shrugged. "It was in the same hands for sixty years. The old lady had no interest in it."

"And now, it's yours. Does that makes you happy? You've got the Glencoe estate whole again at last. Just as you always wanted it." She frowned momentarily. "It was what you wanted, wasn't it?"

He smiled but the light didn't reach his eyes. "*Was*. Yes, it *was* what I'd always wanted." He rummaged in his pocket. "But my reasons for wanting it have changed." He extracted a sheaf of papers, tied together with a piece of rough string.

"Really?" He handed her the papers. They were still

warm from his body. "What are these?" She held them out to him, questioningly.

"The deeds to Blackrock."

She narrowed her gaze but didn't speak.

"For you. It's your home. You loved it. Build yourself another one there."

"But—"

"No buts. It's yours."

"Why? You said yourself you'd been fighting in the courts for years to get the land. Why just throw it away now?"

"I'm not throwing it away, I'm giving it to you. There's only one thing I want now. And that's for you to be happy. I've had plenty of time to think about what you said, and of course you're right. I'm a controlling, stubborn bastard who has no idea how to handle precious things. I understand your reasons for living away from me. I do. But, the worst of it is, I can't promise you anything different. I am who I am. I can't change that, even for you. Even... if I wanted to."

Gemma was stunned. "I've never heard you say so much in one go."

Callum huffed a grim laugh.

"I'm sorry, I'm being flippant, I—"

"You're right," Callum interrupted. "I'm not given to speeches. And you'd probably have to wait a lifetime before you hear another one."

"A lifetime?" They gazed at each other. Neither moved, neither spoke. Eventually Callum looked away as if unable to face the silence any longer. But Gemma's heart was too full to speak. "That's a long time to wait."

"It's too long, isn't it? No-one has a right to ask a lifetime of someone else."

The tears pricked at the back of her eyes. "*You* can ask."

But her words were drowned by a shout from James that made Callum turn away. She saw the tension in his cheek, a slight tic as a muscle moved in his jaw. She'd never seen it before. He'd always been so strong, so sure. He turned to face her.

"Anyway, Gemma, that's all I came for. So...I'd better go."

He began to walk away. She suddenly remembered the papers. "Callum!"

He looked back at her too quickly, expectantly waiting.

"Thanks! Thanks so much for your gift."

He flashed a brief, joyless smile. "You're welcome."

She watched him walk away to join James and Dallas, who'd just arrived for the holiday weekend. Neither of them noticed her, hidden under the wind-swept boughs of a towering pine tree.

Stunned, Gemma couldn't move, just stared at the papers in her hand. She knew how much Callum had wanted that land. After all, that was why he'd married her, wasn't it? She tightened her fist around the papers until the crisp edges crumpled together. She jumped at the sound of Dallas's greeting to Callum. She watched the three brothers embrace each other. The yellow halo of a lamp surrounded all three of the Mackenzies. How could she have been so blind? The Mackenzie brothers were nothing like Paul and his men. Callum and his brothers would always be there for each other, but it wasn't a sign of control, it was a sign of love. And she'd been too scared to see it. But now she could.

She opened her fingers and let the papers unroll on her palm. He'd wanted the land and he'd just given it to her. She'd accused him of being controlling but giving her the gift of the land at Blackrock wasn't controlling. It was handing control to her. He'd handed her the one thing he thought she wanted—the home she'd been wanting, the freedom she'd been yearning for all these years. And here it was. Hers. So why didn't it feel good? She weighed the papers on her palm as if trying to judge their weight. They were papers. It was just land. It didn't represent the home she'd been wanting—merely a place.

There was only one thing—one *person*—she wanted now.


Throughout the evening Gemma kept an anxious eye on Callum. She was scared he'd disappear before she could finish her official duties as hostess of the evening. He'd kept apart from her, giving her the space to talk to the guests Lizzi, her friend who owned the café, had arranged but he hadn't disappeared.

Now, as people drifted away and the café staff began clearing up, Gemma made her way over to him. He was alone. Dallas had returned to Glencoe and James had disappeared. She'd almost reached Callum when she was stopped by someone. She made her excuses but when she'd turned around he was gone.

She grabbed her warm coat and hat off the hook and rushed outside. Good. Callum's car was still parked on the road. He hadn't left yet. But he was nowhere to be seen.

She shivered as she walked along the quiet street towards the lake. He must have gone towards the water. It would have been his instinct to leave the houses, to find his way to the quiet of the land. She came to the end of the road where a swathe of grass, dusted with snow, gleamed in front of the dark lake. He stood, hands thrust deep in his coat pockets, looking up at the snow clouds that periodically dimmed the slender crescent moon and the Milky Way that arced over their heads. She felt his despair as if it were her own.

She pulled the coat tighter around her as she picked her way carefully across the uneven ground toward him. He didn't hear her approach at first. Then his gaze lowered, across the lake towards the dark bulk of the mountains as if aware of someone's presence. Slowly he turned round to face her. His coat was unbuttoned as if he didn't feel the cold. He never had. She kept on walking until she reached him. She placed her hand on his stomach and she felt his muscles tense beneath her touch. Without speaking, she slid it round to his back, pressing it against the warmth of his skin under his jacket as she laid her cheek against his chest and her head against his shoulder.

"Take me home, Callum."

His hand lightly brushed the small of her back. But it was too gentle to be a caress, more a shifting of his hand to accommodate her body. He hadn't understood.

"Home?" He repeated.

"To Glencoe."

She didn't move. Just listened to the quickened beat of his heart and felt her own increase to meet his rhythm, suddenly unsure. Perhaps she'd been wrong, perhaps he'd simply given her the land as a final goodbye. Had she misinterpreted the gift? She gasped and pulled away, looking up at him, trying to read his unreadable features.

But his face, as strong and dear to her as the land around them, was close enough to kiss and soft enough to touch. She reached out and ran her finger down his strong cheekbone and across his chin.

"I'm so sorry, Callum," she gulped, trying in vain to hold back the tears. "I was wrong. I know what I want now."

His eyes searched her face questioningly.

"You." She gripped his jacket lapels into her fist and tugged them to her, until she could feel the heat of his body against hers. "Only you." She pressed her trembling lips together. "I love you, you see."

Callum thrust his fingers into her hair, either side of her face, and pressed his lips to hers. Neither moved, neither breathed, just held their lips gently against each other's. The heat of their mouths contrasted to the icy cold of the first flutter of snowflakes that drifted straight down from the never ending sky. Too soon, Callum pulled away and brushed a snowflake from her nose.

"I love you, Gemma."

She shook her head, choking with tears and laughter. "Really?"

"Of course. I love you. You won't have to wait a lifetime to hear those words again. I'll tell you every day, until you stop doubting me. I love you. I—"

Whatever else he was going to say was lost as she pressed her mouth to his. The stars, the snow and the cold receded until the only reality was the warmth of his body against hers. It told her everything she needed to know to keep her going for a lifetime.

## EPILOGUE

Gemma groaned uncomfortably and shifted as far as the monitor leads would allow her. The doctors had told her it was just a waiting game and she was prepared. She shifted once more to her side, trying to find a place where the pressure of the baby wasn't so painful and took a deep breath, inhaling the scent of the flowers that filled every available space. She gasped as a sharp pain pierced her body.

"Painful?"

She looked into Callum's concerned face. He was more nervous than she was. "Not really," she tried to reassure him. But as another contraction gripped her body she cried out.

"I'll get the doctor."

She lay back and exhaled noisily as the pain passed. "It's okay. Really."

He flicked a lock of hair that was stuck to her damp face and smoothed it between his fingers. "You're so beautiful, Gemma."

"Are you kidding me? I'm in labor, my hair's all over the place, I'm running a temperature and feel nauseous."

"Beautiful," he repeated.

She grimaced, breathed deeply of the gas and air through a mouthpiece, picked up his hand, luxuriating in his strength and his rock steady love, and kissed it. She closed her eyes against the escalating pain, despite the pain relief, trying not to panic. She gripped his hand. "You won't leave me, will you?"

"Of course not."

"Then," she smiled as the panic and pain ebbed away once more, "you must promise me that you'll forget everything you hear me say. There *will* be the use of swear words which you possibly have never heard before and you must forget I've ever said such things."

He kissed her hand in acceptance.

"Then, I may need to bite on something or dig my nails into you if the going gets rough. *That's* what you're here for."

He kissed the inside of her elbow in acceptance.

"Lastly, while I rant and rage, you must soothe me with massages, stroking, words—whatever you can."

He kissed her neck and brought his head close to hers, hesitating, unsure. His eyes lowered in a frown, searching her face.

"You know I'm no good with words. I might need a trial run on that one."

She shifted again. "Just try. Tell me...anything."

"How about 'I'm here for you, always.' Would you find that soothing?"

Tears sprung to her eyes. She sniffed and tried to ignore them. "Short," she nodded, "but soothing. Anything else?"

Callum blew out his cheeks. "Now you're pushing it. I've just about exhausted my romantic repertoire."

The tears rolled down her face. By the look of panic on his face, he must have mistaken her tears for sadness. "Gemma," he gripped her hands tightly. "I can't put what I feel for you in words. You *know* that. I'm too useless with words and, it—how I feel for you—is just too big. It's all of me, it's my life." He paused, his eyes searching around the hospital room, as if for inspiration. But he didn't need it. When he looked back at her, she could see he knew exactly what to say. "*You're* my life. It's that simple."

Gemma eased herself up on her elbows and smiled. She couldn't say anything, her heart was too full.

Callum swallowed. "Say something, Gemma. *You're* good with words."

"Not as good as you." She shook her head. "I can only think of three. I love you, Callum Mackenzie."

"That's five."

Gemma's laughter turned into a cry as another contraction took hold. But through the shroud of pain she could have sworn she heard the words, "I love you, too", whispered against her ear.


"It's a girl," Callum breathed.

Gemma sighed, a bone deep sigh, and brushed the back of her finger along the fine, golden down of her daughter's hair. "Violet Rose."

Callum didn't bat an eyelid. He brought the tightly wrapped bundle to his lips and kissed the top of her head. "Violet Rose, welcome home."

Suddenly the doors flew open and Dallas, Cassandra, Lily and James burst in with balloons and shouts. James popped open a bottle of champagne and Lily, clothed entirely in pink, shrieked when told she had a girl cousin. Dallas kissed Gemma, and Cassandra tried to contain Lily's enthusiasm for her new cousin.

James leaned against the wall, sipped his champagne, and watched a tear that Callum hadn't been able to control, slip down his face. He'd never seen Callum cry before. A baby could make you do that, he guessed. He watched as Callum held his daughter so carefully, cradling her in his arms as if she were the most precious thing in the world. James looked up at the clinical ceiling—white paint, bare strip lighting—willing the swell of sadness to leave him. He swallowed, glanced briefly at his brothers surrounded by children and the women they loved, and quietly left the room.

## AFTERWORD

Thank you for reading *Escape to Shelter Springs*. I hope you enjoyed it! This is the first of my books to introduce the town of Shelter Springs next to Shelter Lake, where two more books in the Mackenzies series are based. Shelter Springs is based on the real South Island town of Tekapo, famous for its lake, its clear night sky and its church, which I used as the location for Callum's and Gemma's wedding.

*Escape to Shelter Springs* is the third book in the Mackenzies series. An excerpt follows of the next book—*What You See in the Stars*—which features Morgan and Rebecca.

A Place Called Home (Guy and Lucia)
Secrets at Parata Bay (Dallas and Cassandra)
Escape to Shelter Springs (Callum and Gemma)
What you See in the Stars (Morgan and Rebecca)
Second Chance at Whisper Creek (James and Susie)
Summer at the Lakehouse Café (Pete and Lizzi)

Sophie

# WHAT YOU SEE IN THE STARS
## BOOK 4 OF THE MACKENZIES—MORGAN

*A nerdy astronomer. A macho cowboy. And a heartache that neither could have seen in the stars...*

Astronomer Rebecca Mayhew has a list of what her eventual

*husband will be like. It's just how she does things. Nice, neat and orderly so as not to disturb the pain of her past which is buried deep.*

*Farmhand Morgan West has a past which is anything but nice and neat, and a present to match. That's why he keeps moving on, never staying long in one place.*

*Trouble is, some things, like love, can derail the best laid plans. And when Rebecca falls hard for Morgan, her nice, neat orderly world unravels and secrets are revealed that have the potential to explode more than just their own worlds.*

## Excerpt

She glanced through the ten points that she required of a potential mate.

- 1. Self-confident (but not arrogant)
- 2. Respectful of women and feminists
- 3. Good career
- 4. Careful with money
- 5. Tall (but not too tall)
- 6. Steady and responsible
- 7. Well-traveled
- 8. Good conversationalist
- 9. Well-educated
- 10. Of neat build (not too slim and not too broad)

All reasonable, or necessary. She wanted someone who would fit in. Someone much like herself. Except taller of course. But not too tall. A logical list. If only people had a more scientific approach she was sure there would be fewer separations, fewer unhappy marriages like her own parents who still lived separate lives in their terraced house in Manchester. No, her list was the only rational approach to finding a husband.

Suddenly the line of Morgan's jaw, lit by the streetlamp, filled her mind, giving her stomach a little flip of desire. This was swiftly followed by her memory of his back, the soft, well-worn shirt pulled across his broad shoulders as he reached over to pick up a beer. And those muscles.

She swallowed. And doodled beside point 10. She hesitated only a moment before crossing it out. Adding 'Strong physique' instead. She'd simply got it wrong. Hadn't considered it sufficiently. Now she'd seen the kind of physique she liked, she could alter her requirements.

Nothing was ever set in stone, after all. Maybe there was room in her life for someone a little different to the man on her list. Maybe she should tweak her list a little over the next few weeks. It's what scientists did with a good hypothesis. Nothing wrong with that.

Find out more!

# ABOUT THE AUTHOR

Hello!

My name is Sophie Haydon and I write romances with stories which make you turn the pages, and characters who feel real.

I'm an avid people watcher, hopeless romantic and dreamer who spends far too much time gazing out the window, imagining scenes where people struggle with life and emotions but always end up happily. Because, yes, I'm also an eternal optimist!

I currently have two connected series — Mackenzies and Lantern Bay — which feature the Mackenzie and Connelly families. At the moment, I'm writing the fifth Lantern Bay book, but am already planning future series.

All the books I've written so far are set in New Zealand, where I live. But I was born on the north Norfolk coast of England and am planning a series set in the small seaside town in which I grew up. And then there's my Nantucket trilogy which I began planning years ago, but have yet to find time to write.

So, wherever you are in the world, welcome to my little corner, where I sit with my two cocker spaniels snoring gently beside me, creating worlds where people struggle with life and emotions but are always rewarded with love and happiness in the end. Because that's non negotiable!

I hope you enjoy my books.

Sophie

x